FOLLOW ME DOWN

FOLLOW

ME

Kio Stark

DOWN

Red Lemonade

a Cursor publishing community

Brooklyn, New York

2011

Library of Congress Cataloging-in-Publication Data
[INSERT CIP DATA]
A portion of this work was originally published,
in slightly different form, in *Cell Stories*.

Cover and interior design by Ian Crowther/Lousy with the Spirit
Printed in the United States of America

Red Lemonade
a Cursor publishing community
Brooklyn, New York

www.redlemona.de

Distributed by Publishers Group West

10 9 8 7 6 5 4 3 2 1

There was a knock at the door and I didn't answer. The same knock, over so many years. The same broken man on the far side of the door, looking for redemption we both know won't hold. When his footsteps faded away, I packed a bag and boarded a bus. Disappearing was easier than I thought it would be.

I arrived here in the heart of night, awakened by the long sigh of the bus as it followed the curved ramp up into the dark cement stable and eased into a narrow berth. I found a room full of sun, on a block with leafy sidewalks, truncated at either end by a well-kept housing project. Nearby is an old, fouled canal. There are bodegas and men loitering on the corners, teenagers taunting each other. Sometimes what you want is to be somewhere you do not belong.

Every day, I pass through the skin of the neighborhood out into the wider world. I am on a journey. I'm a white girl with scarlet hair. I live among strangers. Nobody knows my name.

I'm going outside now. Come with me.

AUGUST

1.

IT'S DUSK ON A SATURDAY, I'm out walking. There's a man, unsteady on his feet, with a long, curled-handle umbrella. He's holding it up to his shoulder like a machine gun, staring down the barrel and swiveling abruptly, a jungle commando, pausing to catch his image in the scratched plexiglass window of the bodega. A small boy wanders out of the store and stands a few feet away, watching. The man pivots slowly, beginning to grunt and growl before he comes around to face the boy. The boy pulls his arms around himself and waits to see where this is going. So do I. The man hunkers down and grunts his way toward the boy, the umbrella-gun carefully aimed. I'm weighing my slightness against the man's new equilibrium. In case. Then, something invisible passes between them and the tension breaks. The boy giggles and runs behind a tree, peeking out. The man pulls a forty-ounce out of a pocket and sits down on the bodega steps. The evening begins.

In the projects, people are milling around, winding up to things that come later. There's a butter-colored Cadillac parked out front. The door rests open and the song on the radio drifts out into the air. A man sits in the car with his feet on the curb. He's wearing one of those old man caps, and seems old enough to have earned it. He sings past the volume of the radio, his voice fluid, with just a little gravel in it. I smile at him, and he tips his hat. "That's right, baby," he says and meets up with the song again on a high, trailing note.

A few blocks away a man is leaning back against the side of his sedan, one arm stretched out above the door as though the car were his best girl. There's a mambo playing, and all around the men are lifting beers swaddled in brown paper and shimmying in place, their heads thrown back with pleasure. Now he reaches into his pocket and scatters a handful of bright pennies in the empty street. A few small children rush over at the sound of fallen coins, squatting to gather them. He watches with pride at what he has caused. The other men keep dancing in place as the song changes key.

When full darkness settles in, the corner boys are practicing footwork with invisible basketballs, pivoting around each other. One takes a jump shot and his gaze follows it up to the shining moon. "Yo," he says, "is the moon a planet?" He's looking at the smallest of the boys, the wiry one who must be the answer man among them. Answer Man says, "The moon's name is Maria."

There's a girl, I haven't seen her since midsummer. Now she steps out her front door. Something has changed. She has grown into herself. She stretches and yawns, and takes her time settling down to sit on the top step. She tips her head one way, and then the other. She is utterly self-contained. Not fidgeting, not posing, not waiting. After a while the boys come slowly out of the dark, one by one. They sit at her feet and ignore each other. She gives the street an idle scan. Minutes pass. Nobody says a word.

The world is beautiful but I am not quite in it. I walk back home through the projects, there are flashing lights all around, ambulances and idling rigs. The firemen lumber under the weight of their gear. People on corners are spreading the news. Something has happened and these are the artifacts left behind by the thing that has happened. EMTs lean around an empty gurney on a pathway. Whatever went wrong has been taken away. In the middle of the courtyard lawn, one man in flannel pajamas and a do-rag stands and counts a handful of change.

—

I had a brother once. That last time he knocked on my door, I didn't answer. He had been the light in my eyes, an earnest and unprotected boy, foolish and charming. I lost him to the city. The last time he knocked on my door was the day I left him behind.

———

On Sundays the whole neighborhood sleeps late. There must have been rain at dawn, for now the streets and the trees have taken on the darker hue and shimmer that the water leaves on their surfaces as it evaporates back into the sky. All the colors are rich and saturated, the peeling bark of the birches, the green weeds, the mangled red tricycle that sits on the curb awaiting the trashmen's visit. I spool a roll of film into one of my old plastic toy cameras. It's light and imprecise. My cameras are a good excuse to see the neighborhood, to stop and stare. The camera opens a space for that, and people always ask what I'm doing. They are puzzled, by the antiquated equipment and the things they see me shooting: the buildings and the places where the buildings used to be. The surface of the canal, lambent with marbled oil. The trees and weeds overtaking the things that man has left in his wake.

This morning I go first to the playground. There's a young woman there who I know a little, Carlina. She's tall and curvy and her clothes are always sculpted to set her roundness at best advantage. Even when she's in sweats, as she is now. She's watching her son, who is in constant motion, circling the playground and mounting its obstacles. He's around six, I think. She waves. "You're taking pictures again? What's up with that?"

She asks me that every time she sees me with a camera. At first I tried to explain, I showed her some prints. But that's not really what her questions are about. It's the meaningless but meaningful conversation of the street. She is acknowledging me as familiar, as a known quantity. I return the gesture. "You guys are out early."

"He's hit a new surge of testosterone or something. If I don't take him out and run him in the morning he's hell all day long. Swings at everybody. Gets all pent-up and sinks his teeth in another kid's arm. Jesus, men. You know?"

Take him out and run him. Like a dog or a horse. I just nod. Then I have an idea. I set the camera down on the flat edge of a bench and point it at the jungle gym, the speeding boy. I hold the shutter open for a long time, maybe a minute. The picture will be washed out with light, the physical structures barely visible. And the boy will be a blurred streak of motion, pure energy and light. I try it a few times, varying the time the shutter is open.

The boy's mother turns away to take a phone call. She seems uncomfortable, tries to hustle the caller off the phone. "I'm not in a good place to talk. We're outside. Hold on."

She turns to me. "Can you watch him? I just have to deal with something." She taps the phone. "Ten minutes. It's one of those kind of delicate matters, you know?"

No problem, I tell her. I load another roll of film and keep shooting the boy's flashing speed. When she comes back, he's hanging upside-down from the monkey bars, resting. She hollers him over, in the commanding tone of mothers and generals. It works. He drops down and trots to her side. She waves at me. "Thanks," she says and turns quickly back into the tall housing project building she lives in. I wait a while, watching, hoping for a rustle at a window that will show me which apartment is hers. But nothing happens. Eventually I move on.

I loop through the neighborhood, down by the canal and back. When I get home, my lover Jimmy is sitting on the stoop. He doesn't like phones, he is undaunted by waiting. "I was in the neighborhood," is what he says every time I find him like this. It's a joke that's always funny. He lives four blocks away.

He slides a hand around my calf as I climb the steps, and stands up to follow me into the house. I turn on the ceiling fans and a breeze picks up through the apartment, from the kitchen's wide back windows out to the narrower ones overlooking the street.

In my living room, a mosaic of photographs covers one long wall. I add a few new ones every week or so, and I shuffle them around, reworking the schemes, seeing which rules make better compositions. Jimmy stands in front of the wall now, giving it his fullest scrutiny.

"You changed it. It's by dominant color," he observes, pointing at the wall. "The green of the plants. The gray of the fences and the empty buildings. The red of the bricks and the rust."

"I think it's too much," I say.

"Too much how?"

"Too obvious." I step back and consider the wall a moment. I don't like the workings of my mind to be so easy to guess, but that's only part of my discomfort. "You don't see the pictures anymore, just a field of color. It blinds the eye to detail."

"Never any people," Jimmy says. It's not the first time he's observed this, and he's pleased with himself.

"People are only interesting to me in motion," I tell him. "But that's not really why. This is about a world without people at all. After people. That's what all these are," I tell him. I'm pacing now in front of the wall, pointing, caught up in my own convictions. "These are the ruins we leave behind. The foolish pride of our skyscrapers and our factories, left empty and grown over with weeds."

Jimmy sits down on the couch while I'm talking, and looks up at me, a little confused, a little smitten. "They're pictures of impermanence," he says, working it out. "You're taking pictures of an idea."

I chose Jimmy because I thought he was someone else. A nice guy who plays guitar and doesn't think too hard about things. I had him all wrong, and that complicates my hours with him in a way that makes me shrink into myself. I suppress the uneasy feeling by kneeling down and unzipping his pants.

—

Early Monday morning, I'm hustling to the subway, squinting in the brightness. A man is sitting on an upturned milk crate, drinking coffee from a mug. He raises it in greeting. The incongruity of the street perch and the kitchen cup pull a grin out of me. He shakes his head. "A man could look at a smile like that for the rest of his life," he says. I stop a moment. I like the look of this one. He's got some Cherokee around the eyes, a lullaby voice, the rangy arms of a swimmer. He rocks a little on the milk crate, then holds out the mug. "Want a sip?" I'm late for work, the air is thick as a swamp. I laugh, and keep walking.

The city is shifting, it blurs, and then reforms itself whenever my back is turned. Now, I cut through an old neighborhood where the punks and squatters used to reign. Every time I come down here, something else is gone. This morning a man with a fine-boned face and an untucked shirt walks toward me, his arm angled out like a dandy's. He comes closer and I see that he's crying in a dry and quiet way as he walks, the face quivering and the eyes ringed red. Up close the cocked arm seems to be holding him up, no longer a flourish. It's so early in the morning, it all bespeaks heartbreak. A final night, a last, fumbling exit, a sorrow that sinks like a stone.

It's not just him. Everyone here is maimed. A pimply girl shuffles along, her head tipping back like a narcoleptic, she is nodding on something, coming unwound with each step. There's a man dragging his leg along behind him like an unwanted burden. Then a skinny guy in high-tops with breasts bouncing under his t-shirt rushes into one of the doorways. A round woman who guides her electric wheelchair with flipper limbs whirs past an old man with a bandage around his neck like an ascot. An elegant woman with upswept hair and three fingers in a claw-shaped cast is telling a story to no one. Then the nodding girl doubles back, tucks herself into the shade of a ghetto palm and gives in to the sleep she can't outrun.

I keep walking, as if motion might erase the morning's purgatorial characters from my imagination. Now I'm really late, and a soft rain has begun to fall. I catch the express and arrive at the tallest building by the river, where I'm employed by an immense law firm. In the lobby, a janitor is rolling out a fresh mud rug. It still curls upward at the corners. He holds one down with his foot and looks sadly at the gray nap. It's temporary, disposable. It's there to protect the granite floors. But I think he looks at its fresh surface and sees only the coming loss. It will never be this perfect, this clean, again.

Upstairs on the highest floor is the dead zone, where I work. The colors are pale, all blonde wood and warm white paint. The spareness is only casually marred by personal clutter, against regulation. Otherwise it's bloodless. From the window of my small room here, I can see the tips of a few buildings and miles of sky. The weather turns my mood as it changes the light across my desk. Flat and gray, bright and blinding. I am a proofreader. I look for mistakes. I gather errors. On the corner of my desk, there's a stack of papers in a tray. I go through them, mark changes. The assistant comes to pick up the finished ones. She's a little wobbly, with solid flesh rolling over the waist of her skirt, heels too high and narrow to support her width. But it's not just the body, she's a wobbly person. She lacks purpose. She wants to ask me questions, and she never does. She stands in the doorway watching, waiting for an invitation that never comes. I turn back to the window. I hear her breathing. I hear her finally turn and go, her heels clicking on the wooden floor like a 1950s starlet's would. She never asks the things she wants to ask. No one here does. They used to. But I don't talk.

On my way home, the subway is full of rancid energy, a collective bad mood, as if something might snap any second. I get off and wait for the next train. It's better here, languid. First a woman stretches her arms out behind her and groans a little, releasing the day from her shoulders, pulling her shirt tight across her lovely round breasts. Then another woman shifts her weight and the waist of her skirt slides down past the knob of her hip, revealing a crescent of pale flesh. An Asian man with a boyish face and an elegant suit averts his eyes, shaking his head and smiling with incredulity at these wonders, and how he is expected to act as though he does not see them.

When I come back above ground into the closing day, a tall guy says to me, "You're a beautiful lady, you just made my day walkin' by here."

Little guy crossing the street says, "Mine too."

Tall guy calls out to him, "Right? You work all day, you deserve to see something beautiful."

Little guy says, "It's like the icing."

By the high school, there are six antsy cops guarding the corners against some sinister potential I can't perceive. The kids are milling around on the sidewalks. They've all grown great pillows of fat since I saw them last, it spills out of their tight clothes, and now their bodies take up as much of the sidewalk as their voices.

Around the corner on a side street, some girls are jumping Double Dutch, thump-thump, thump-thump, thump-thump, thump, "Ice cream soda pop cherries on top / how many boyfriends do you got?"

—

The next night at home I put on higher heels and lipstick and run back out to meet Natalie. She's got an opening tonight. When I first arrived, I had a temp job proofing at the newspaper where Natalie works as a news photographer, and I have come to count on the balance of her rational view of the world, her calculated eye. Photojournalism happens on the street, but Natalie's gallery work is something entirely different. It's the earth itself, the soil and the empty surface of the land, shot from distances that can't be measured. It's topographic and mathematical. It soothes me.

The gallery is a far walk from the train. I pass a couple arguing. His voice breaks like a boy's as he says, "Yeah, and what exactly did you do about it?" She stands silent, her head tipped away from him, chin askew. There's nothing so impassable about her, but you can tell she's going to win.

Out in front, in the soft, misty rain, people are smoking and talking with their hands. A very small woman in a curvy black dress is standing alone with her arms crossed, shiny black curls swinging around her bare shoulders. The man next to me says hello to her, and then to me. She smiles at both of us, it's a friendly night, here in the rain. She seems both relieved and dismayed to have been noticed as a person who is waiting for something. I ask her why she's standing around.

"My friend is very very late," she tells me. Her shoulders rise and drop, punctuating her annoyance. She holds a palm up to the rain. She's tapping her foot. She's smiling through all of this. She's performing something.

"You could wait inside," I say, pointing at the massive plate glass windows that separate us from the party.

"Oh no," she says. "I want to stay here and get even madder by the time he shows up."

Now I get it. Now I'm interested. "What are you going to say when he does?"

She gives me a look that says, we're in this together, we women, we know how this works, we know where the power lies. "I'm going to tell him," she leans closer, "that he better buy me a drink before I'll even say a word to him."

We both laugh, and she whisks some of the dewdrops off her pretty arms. A taxi pulls up, a man in a nice shirt and nice shoes tumbles out. He seems earnest even in the way he unfolds himself from the taxi, eager and clumsy. It's not what I expected at all. I look back at her, she winks at me as he brushes past me to greet her.

Over my shoulder, I can hear her. She's not mad at all.

I go in. The photographs are rich and dense. They're massive prints from a large-format camera. This set is a series of aerial shots, taken from the helicopter her father flies out West, scouting for fires. "The land as it was never meant to be seen," that's how she describes the patterns her camera has found. "We see it from planes all the time, but in motion. The stopped shot jars me. I think about how only people who could climb high mountains ever saw anything resembling this. Until hot-air balloons. And then, everything about the way we mapped space changed. In the 19th century there are beautiful maps, they're called panoramas, because they show three-dimensional space. The world seen from above." She's been saying all this to me since the project began, and now I hear her saying it to a couple with perfectly glowing skin. Buyers. Natalie's voice gets a little bigger, a little deeper, when she's performing herself. I know that if she catches my eye, she'll falter. I cross the room to get some wine and hover by one of my favorite images, a village in a valley between two tall peaks, hidden, protected. Natalie pushes the crowd aside with her shoulder and comes to me.

"Are they buying?"

She's grinning, standing on tiptoes like a little girl. "The show just sold out."

"Really? That's wonderful."

She pulls me across the room to where her gallerist is holding court. She tugs his perfectly tailored jacket sleeve. "George, this is Lucy." He takes my hand and raises it to his lips, leaves a soft kiss there. "Ah, the best friend, lovely to meet you," he says. I work hard to still the slight pinch that always comes into my expression when I hear my name aloud. It's the wrong name, the name of a woman who is softer around the edges than I am, more generous, more graceful. I live with the disjuncture, I am too honest to change it. Without a trace of rudeness, the gallerist lets his attention glide back to the big spenders he's turned away from to greet me. Natalie leans over my glass of wine and smacks my cheek with a kiss. "I have to go out with the gallery people and some of the clients after. You'll come?"

"No, no. I have to get home." She doesn't often tolerate refusals, but success has her dazzled and my words evaporate before she can take umbrage. I squeeze her shoulder and watch her return to her gallerist's side. From a few paces away I can really take him in. His suit is so elegant I want to slide inside it with him.

When I get back to the neighborhood, there's Dealer on his corner. The one who always says hello. He's management, you can tell because he's never drunk on the job. This time I walk by and one of his boys says, "Got a fine ass on her." Dealer thwacks the boy's hat off his head and says, "Don't talk about her like that, she *nice.*"

I cross the courtyard of the projects, passing by people leaning back on the benches in the darkness left by the busted streetlamps. They're just forms in the night, murmuring. From a bench I've just passed, a man hisses softly and says, "You don't know me anymore?" I stop. It's the wrong voice, but that's Dealer's line. This one speaks with a little dust of malice, nothing like Dealer's sweetness, the way you can hear his smile from behind your back.

It's the bind of living here. If I don't turn around and let him flirt with me, I'm a bitch. If I do turn around, there's an invitation in the gesture that I don't mean at all, that doesn't feel safe in the deep darkness of the listless night.

So I do what I always do. I turn around anyway. "Do I know you?" I ask, walking toward him and his boys on the bench, leaning forward to squint at his face.

"I'm Georgie," he says. "Come on. Don't you know me?" But he can't keep the grin down. He's just marking time in the night.

"Your name's not Georgie," I say, laughing now. "I never saw you before in my life."

He taps his feet and his hand forms a thumbs-up gun. He cocks and shoots. "I gotcha though," he says. "Didn't I just?"

"You sure did." I'm turning back toward home. "Have a good night."

"That's right girl, you just sashay on home now," he says, and one of his friends whistles long and low.

2.

A WEEK AFTER NATALIE'S OPENING, I get home from work late in the evening and the whole neighborhood is out in the street. Carlina is down on the corner in a bathing suit and shorts, her waist like the curve of a guitar. She's fanning herself with a newspaper and talking to Julio, a short guy who watches over the corner. He's got a big belly, an incongruous handlebar mustache. He's always smiling but I don't buy it at all. Now there's music playing softly from someone's open window. Julio and Carlina wave at me as I stand in the doorway shuffling through the mail. There's an envelope that doesn't belong here. It's to "Hombre Cinco," and it isn't my address. I look closer. It's dirty, the stamp is years out of date, the canceling marks are illegible now, there's no way to know when it was mailed. It must have been rescued from the dungeon of a dead letter office.

I should give it back to the postman. But I don't.

The address on the envelope isn't far away. A few blocks, down by the canal. But it's just off the industrial street where the whores walk at night. I go upstairs and look out the back window at the red moon rising over the decaying water tower.

By the time I get out the door the next day, Julio's already watching the corner, under cover of the burnt-out store's fiberglass awning. "Hello mami," he calls out. "You go to work?"

"Just a walk," I tell him. I don't like to linger with Julio. He starts asking questions. Who is my boyfriend and do I need any help around the house. I hurry down the street that fronts the canal, the whores have gone home and it's empty now, there's only broken glass and the leftover stench of the garbage trucks.

The address I'm looking for is on a stub of a street, half a block long, cut short by the canal and a yellow diamond sign that says, simply, "END."

There's a sofa near the drooping fence that borders the canal. A man rises from it and staggers up to me. "Look at that face. I'm gonna marry you. I'm gonna buy you an apart—no, a house. Gonna get a job, go back to school. Okay?"

"Okay," I say, backing away from the sour stink of him. There's no one else around. Even Julio is too far away to help me. The man keeps walking, muttering to himself.

He lurches away toward the empty park. When he's out of sight, I turn back to the little street. One side is the solid wall of a warehouse, casement windows behind cast iron cages. The other side has three little townhouses with ugly siding, dirty white, hospital green, mud brown. I count the house numbers. Where a fourth would be, at the end of the street, is an empty lot. That's the one I'm looking for.

I go down and grab the big steel lock that binds the gates with a rusty chain, rattle it a little, hoping it might give. It holds fast. The lot is narrow and deep. The pavement is going to seed as grass and weeds push up through the cracked blacktop. Ivy snakes through the links of the cyclone fence and into the razor wire that crowns it. There's a great sprawling Paulownia tree shading the back, and smaller ones pushing up all around the edges, growing out of the paltry, toxic dirt. Those trees grow fast, but still, the lot must have been vacant for decades.

Maybe that's all there is to it.

I keep the letter in my pocket and head for the post office. My fingers graze its surface, feeling the grit collected in its limbo years.

The line is long and slow. There's a man up near the front of the impatient crowd, rocking a sleeping baby back and forth in a cheap stroller. He's got the blackest hair and his skin is rosy brown. Finally it's his turn, and there's something a little frightened in the way he approaches the window. He's holding out a tissuey paper, a carbon of some kind of official form. His words are soft and incomplete as he says to the clerk, "I need a photocopy. Can I do here?" She shakes her head. "No?" he asks, still a little hopeful. "I can not do that here?" The clerk waves him away.

He turns the stroller around and wheels it slowly toward the door. He's looking at the paper in his hand. He's navigating strange territory, things don't work the way they work at home. He's almost at the door when a fat woman steps out of the line, clucking her tongue at the whole situation. "Over there," she tells him, pointing out the window. "Across the street at the Arab store. They do it." She pats him on the arm. "Just cross the street, honey."

I would swear he is about to cry. The moment is frozen. I'm still six or seven people from the clerk's window. I touch the letter in my pocket. I step out of the line. I'm keeping a secret I meant to turn loose. I hurry toward the door, just in time to hold it open for the man and his stroller. Up close I see it's not tears he's holding back. It's rage.

The letter stays in my bag all day at work. At night, in my kitchen, I stare at the stove. It would be so simple. But a little steam and suddenly you're a felon. I'm not sure yet. I slide the envelope between two fingers and feel the edges of something less pliable than the worn paper. It's a rectangle with rounded edges. Thicker and smaller than a folded letter. A photograph.

My phone rings, and I pin the envelope onto the fridge with a tiny magnet, adding it to the haphazard collage of scraps and postcards. It works the wrong way, I always forget. Display a thing and it becomes invisible.

SEPTEMBER

3.

I STOP FOR COFFEE on the way to work. There's an old woman at one of the tables, dressed in red and gold, her hair as delicate as spun sugar. Her hands are gnarled with arthritis, curled like claws. She's eating a raspberry jam cookie, resting from time to time. Some part of consuming the treat is costing her effort. A young blond man in a blue blazer comes in, and she's momentarily captivated. Maybe he's a ghost to her, someone from her youth, or maybe she's never stopped looking wistfully at young men. When she packs up to leave, she stops a slick Asian guy with bleached hair and asks if he knows the buses in the neighborhood. He doesn't.

On the subway, everyone's in the quiet space between what came before and what comes next. There's a tall fat man with a cheap cane and worried eyes. Nearby a young man is leaning against the pole, trying to suppress the inward, private smile that keeps overtaking his face. An older woman with veined hands notices a small stain on her pink pants, touches it as though that might give her new information, then moves her purse to conceal it. She reads over my shoulder for a while, and then her head drops down into sleep. The smiler gets off near the university, the fat man at the railway station. The dozing woman, I imagine, keeps dozing all the way up the line.

In Midtown near my office, there is a man who is paid to vacuum the wide slate sidewalks surrounding the modernist skyscraper every morning. He never smiles.

My day in the dead zone is long. It's late by the time I can leave work, a deadline, other people have failed and it all falls to me. I have forgotten to eat. I feel the vertigo of nausea without the threat of retching. I can't face the subway, it will unravel me. I hail a cab. When we pull up in front of my house, the driver says, "Is this a safe neighborhood?" I tell him yes. He says, "Are you sure? It looks a little... heavy."

As if to illustrate the driver's point, as I'm slamming the door, a man walks toward me, fast like he wanted some distance between him and what's behind him. His face has an addict's ashen cast, the skin loose over the insistent bones, and for a slippery moment what I see is my brother, bearing down the street toward me. The vision clears before I can react. The man shakes his head, I can see the greasy tendrils of his hair bouncing. He passes me, looks back over his shoulder, and then mutters decisively, "Man, I quit. I fucking quit."

4.

EVERYTHING THAT HAPPENS, happens on the street. One lazy afternoon when I first came to the city, I found an old, inlaid chest of drawers at a stoop sale. It was in good shape, perfect dovetail joints. They wanted a hundred for it, and I knew it was worth a lot more. I looked in the windows of their brownstone and saw the spare minimalism of the living room. White furniture with hard angles. They'd changed their style and they wanted the evidence hauled away quickly, they wanted this more than they cared about recouping the costs of their changed taste. The transaction was quick, I gave them $80, and saw how easily they expanded their loss by a small increment. Just take it away, they were thinking. I borrowed a hand truck from the bodega and started dragging the large piece home. A man saw me coming and stepped out of my way, then seemed to think better of it, turned back and asked if I need help. "I'm okay," I said. All I can think when men offer to carry things for me is: and then what would I owe you.

He watched me a moment, struggling with the bulk of my burden. "Are you sure?" And without waiting for an answer, he took two quick steps toward me and reached a skinny arm out for the handle of the hand truck. I liked that he could act and hesitate in the same broad gesture. I let him take it.

He carried it up the stairs for me. I gave him a beer. His name is Jimmy, he told me. We pulled two chairs up to the front window and propped our feet up on the sill, looking down on the street while we talked. I liked him. He was gangly and honest. His voice was stronger than his body looked.

"Where did you come from?"

He smiled. It took a long time to reach its fullness. His chin cocked sideways a little and his teeth peeked out over his bottom lip. One tooth crossed over the other slightly. What's imperfect is beautiful. What's imperfect is alive. "I could be from here," he said.

"But you're not."

"How do you know?"

"Statistically probable. Almost no one is really from here." What I said is true, but it's not really how I knew. He moves like molasses, slow and sensual. I knew he was from somewhere else, and he hadn't been here long. The city hadn't broken his languor yet.

"Down south."

"Why did you leave?"

He leaned toward me and clinked his beer bottle against mine. "I followed a girl, but that didn't come out so well."

"But you stayed."

"I'm a proud man. I didn't want her to know that was why."

"What did you tell her?"

"Well, I play guitar. A buddy of mine had been after me to come up and play with his band for a while. I kept saying no, and then I said yes. Pretty easy."

I looked at his fingers. They were long and graceful. "Bass guitar, right?"

"You're pretty good at this."

I gave him a coy shrug. He didn't know the half of it. "So how's the band?"

"Good. We're recording in a few months. Just practicing now, but I like what I hear."

"What does a Monday look like for you?"

"I sleep late. I take the subway. I fix guitars."

"Talented fingers," I said, without meaning the innuendo. We both let it sit for a while. I got up to get more beer. He shifted his long legs, crossing at the ankles.

When I came back, he took the beer, our fingers sliding together around the sweaty bottle. "What about you?"

"Can you be more specific?"

"Monday."

"I get up early. I go to Midtown to a big office. I spend too much time watching people on the way to the subway. I get distracted, I end up late. No one complains."

"What happens at the office?"

"I hunt for mistakes."

"That's pretty big game."

"Pretty small, more like it. Miniscule game."

"Are you good at it?"

"Very good."

"I bet."

I looked out the window into the middle distance, the windows across the street, the near rooftops. I could feel Jimmy watching me. It was hot, my cheeks flushed with the beer and the attention. Jimmy tipped his chair back a little, settling into the fulsome quiet between us. He set his empty bottle on the floor. The light began to fade. We were sweating in the dusk, his warm brown skin glimmering with it. A breeze picked up and stirred the edges of the drawn curtain. I'd been alone a long time then. I didn't remember how it worked. I stood up, and Jimmy did too.

"I should go," he said. "You must have stuff to do."

I didn't say anything. I could feel my smile, it was crooked and mischievous. Why not, I thought. What I said to Jimmy is this: "Take off your clothes."

He let out his held breath in a sputtering laugh.

"I mean it," I said.

So he did.

—

Jimmy wants promises I can't make. Promises are anchors, luxuries. He grows sullen when he runs up against my resistance. Now, he's in my kitchen, it's late evening, he turns his back to me and faces the fridge. It's that gesture, a petty refusal, his weight shifted onto one hip. Jimmy is waiting for me to say something, something like the things he wants to hear, but I outwait him. He gives. He reaches out and plucks the forgotten envelope from under its magnet. "What's this?"

I realize it's been there for weeks, I'd been seeing it and not seeing it every time I opened the fridge. "It's a wrong number," I tell him.

"You didn't put it back in the mail?"

"I keep forgetting."

"I'll do it." He's about to slide it in his back pocket. Before I can think about it, I've snatched it from his hand. He looks at me like I'm an imposter. "I have to go," he says, and I lock the door behind him.

In the morning, I go to the library. The building, constructed in an era of ornate gestures, is an act of generosity, an excess of money made manifest. The broad, shallow steps make an auditorium for people who watch each other idling. Today there are tourists in their bright clothes, smokers leaning back on their elbows, one couple kissing and a man whose head hangs down, maybe he's weary or maybe it's shame. Only his eyes could tell me. I watch him a while but he never looks up.

I go through the heavy revolving doors into the splendid lobby, all tile and gilt. Upstairs on the second floor is the room I'm looking for, where the research librarians work. The room is small, with light filtering in through the back windows. There is a wooden worktable on either side of the room, where people wait for answers. One man is sleeping on his books, and a girl in pearls is writing neatly in a notebook, copying something out of an oversized book splayed open next to her. Beyond the worktables, the room is divided by a mahogany counter, and as I approach it I can just see that behind it the room extends further on either side, a vast machine.

The librarian doesn't look like a librarian at all. Her hair is pulled back in a thick grey-flecked ponytail and she's leaning on her elbows, chin propped neatly in the cleft of her two fists, staring idly into the distance. She smiles as I come closer, and I can see by the crinkles of her eyes that she's close to sixty. She is merry and welcoming, and she's wearing a child's necklace of tiny square wooden beads.

"You look like you have a good question for me," she says, stepping back a bit.

"I do," I tell her.

"Well, try me."

I've been here twice before. What's wonderful is not so much that the librarians can simply walk over to a shelf and pull the exact book that answers your questions. They can do that. But often the answers are already in their heads. They are the keepers of the facts, and I wonder how they memorize the things they know by heart.

"I need to know about dead letter offices. How they work. What happens to the things that end up there."

She perches on her stool. She knows this one without the books. She rolls up her sleeves and looks pleased with herself. She's getting ready to tell me a story, to dazzle me with details. "The dead letter office as an institution is almost as old as the government postal service itself."

"Why does it exist?"

"It was illegal for anyone—and still is, mind you—to open a piece of mail unless they were an employee of the dead letter office. So not even the postmen can. Addresses were less standardized then, a great deal of mail went astray, and some of it held valuable things. Money, jewels."

"People would mail those?"

"There wasn't an option, really, other than a private carrier. Expensive." She leans close. "Get this, it's a hoot. In the old days they hired retired clergy. More trustworthy, they thought. With the money and the jewels and all."

"That's great."

"I doubt that logic would fly these days, what do you think?"

"No, we're all corrupt now, aren't we."

She looks at me a moment, considering the degree of my corruption. "So things that are mailed go astray. Any complex system generates failures. Perhaps the address of the sender and intended recipient are illegible, or misspelled. There can be quite radical misspellings. Phonetics from languages with different alphabets. A mess, you can imagine. These are routed to the dead letter office, and the clerks there try to decipher at least one of the addresses. If they can't, they open it and see if there's any identifying information inside. These people are remarkable, their detective work. If there's still nothing to be done, they store the item in hopes that either the sender or recipient files a claim."

"How long do they keep things?"

"As I understand it, that's a very subjective decision. They keep sentimental items, items of value, much longer. Eventually letters are destroyed and goods are auctioned off."

"Let's say it's a letter."

"I'd guess a year at the most. I'd have to call to verify that." She wags a finger at me, happily. "You've tripped me up!"

I laugh. "Any chance it could be longer?"

"Love letters yes, I'd think so. It's hard to throw love away."

"So it's not like something could be lost for a long time and then redelivered."

Her eyes have gone sly. "So you're talking about a specific item?"

My instinct is to hide it from her, but there's no reason to be covert. "Yes. I got a letter that must be twenty years old. For someone else."

"I see, that *is* interesting. What do *you* think happened?"

All this time I've imagined the letter mislaid, slipped through the cracks of a desk, jammed at the back of a drawer and suddenly freed, sent along its way. I tell her that. She nods as I talk.

"You've definitely got a strange case there." She picks up the phone. "Shall we call them and inquire?"

I shake my head. "No, no. It's fine. I already put it back in the mail."

"You were curious enough to come here, but you don't want to call them."

"I was just walking by. It was a lark. I don't want to bother anyone."

She sizes me up one last time. She resumes her soda fountain pose. "I don't believe a word of that." The look in her eyes halts me from backing away. It's meant to. She picks up the phone again. Someone answers, puts her on hold. She tips the phone away from her ear, impatient, rolling her eyes at me in collusion. The tinny hold music binds us to the phone, and then a voice comes on. She snaps the handset back to her ear, explains the situation, and she holds the phone out to me.

I shake my head.

"Go on," she says. "It's your answer on the other end here, not mine."

I take the phone and say hello.

It's a woman's voice, gruff in a way that suggests years of smoking. "I understand you received a very old letter."

"Yes, I put it back in the mail."

"That's fine. Is that all you need?"

"No," I hesitate. The librarian is tapping her fingers on the counter. "I wanted to know how it could have stayed in the system for all that time. I thought you destroyed things." Satisfied with my progress, the librarian pulls a laptop out of a drawer and turns her attention to it.

"We do. It's possible that one of the inspectors saved it. Had it been opened? Was it a love letter? Everyone has a hard time putting those in the shredder."

"It was still sealed. I don't know what was in it."

"I've never seen anything like that. Your guess is as good as mine, honestly. Was this recently?"

"A few weeks ago."

"We only have a handful of inspectors here. What was the return address?"

"There wasn't one."

"Hm. So it could have come from anywhere. Still, I'll ask the inspectors if any of them remember it. I'd think they would, something that old."

For some reason I don't want to know any more. I don't understand my own reluctance. But there it is. I give her the wrong phone number and hang up.

The librarian turns away from her computer. "Well that was fun, right? Call and let me know what they find out." She hands me her card. I walk down the stairs and out onto the street. I toss her card in the first trashcan I see.

On the subway home, there's a fat girl with a hauntingly beautiful face. She laughs like clear water at something her pug-faced friend says. She looks at him with such open longing, and he turns to stare out the window into the dark tunnel. This can't end well.

Back at home, I lay the envelope on the Formica counter and put the kettle on. Now that I've decided, the act itself is nothing. I hold the envelope over the steam, wave it back and forth a little. Nothing changes. I keep it steady. The ends of the envelope curl upward. I check again.

The glue is still holding fast, the steam keeps nipping my fingertips. It takes a long time before the glue softens, and I can delicately pry up the flap. I think about archeologists unearthing their treasures with toothbrushes.

There's nothing inside but the photograph. I slide it out of the envelope. It's warm from its bath in the steam, curled a little at the edges. The surface is matte, the colors faded. It's old, maybe twenty years, maybe more, the head and shoulders of a young man, shot from below, his hair lifted by the wind. He's tanned and smiling, a little smug. His t-shirt is dirty white. He has good shoulders. His face is bony, he's got a goatee and his blue eyes are bluer than the sky behind him.

On the back, there's something written in dark pencil, smudged. What it says is this: "He has it."

I lean out the kitchen window into the night's heat. The little street where the letter was supposed to go is over there, past the roof of the chop shop, past the windowless factory and its decaying wooden water tower. A train slips across the elevated tracks a mile away. I've been looking out this window for a year. But now it's different. Now I'm looking for something.

The thing is, I don't know what I'm looking for.

But I know where to start. In the morning I put on the red dress. I take an early lunch from work and walk across town as fast as my high heels will allow. On a crowded corner there's a young man with tight shoulders and clipped hair. Tourists surround him but he doesn't see them, he's staring out across the street into the far distance of his imagination. His hands are moving in a pattern that repeats, it seems for a moment like the signs of the cross: Father, Son, Holy Ghost. But it's not, the motions are more intricate and subtle. He flicks two fingers at his chin, and suddenly I see that his fingers are talking, it's sign language, and by the long stare it is clear that his hands are talking to himself. He says the same thing over and over until at last the light changes and his hands drop to his sides, his fingers still moving like pistons, muttering at the sidewalk.

I get there faster than I expected. The classical facade, columns and arches, belies the linoleum and fluorescent interiors of City Hall. The City Clerk's office is in the basement.

The clerk is a fat man, the buttons of his white shirt straining across his belly. He leans on one elbow and looks me over. "Well. What can I do for you?"

I hand him an index card with the address. "Can you tell me who owns this, who used to own it before that? It's an empty lot now."

He turns away and types something into his computer. The keyboard is old. The keys click. "It's in arrears," he says. "Looks like the owner defaulted on the loans. The bank's got it back."

That's no help. "Who defaulted?"

"That's not here, this is the current tax rolls." He leans back in the creaky office chair, his meaty arms behind his head.

This is what the red dress is for. I shift a little, making sure he's got a good view. "How do I find out?"

He shakes his head. "I'd have to pull the deed."

I lean a little further over the counter. "How long does that take?"

"If the bank took it over in the past few years, it's just in the archive here." He jerks a thumb behind him. He's not giving an inch.

"Listen, it sounds like it's extra work for you, I hate to ask. But."

He's waiting.

"It's important."

"Why?"

"I'm looking for something."

"What are you looking for?"

I sigh. "I'm not sure."

He sits up. "Let me get this straight. You want me to go back in that mess and see if I can find a deed for a building that doesn't exist and you don't know why."

"Yes."

He puts his head in his hands. Slowly he pulls his unwieldy body up out of the chair. "It's a nice dress," he says as he walks back toward the door to the archive. His shoes squeak. I hear the sound receding, imagine him walking back through yards and yards of grey metal filing cabinets, heavy with dust. He's been gone a while when the office door opens and a couple comes in. They sit down in the waiting chairs. They are old and weathered and small. His face shines with a permanent grin, even his eyes smile. She is stern, stares back at me, officiously rearranges the contents of her purse. He leans his big head toward her ear and whispers something. She reaches into the purse again and pulls out a hard candy. His face brightens.

I hear the clerk's shoes approaching, and then his bulk moves back through the archive door. His hands are empty. He swipes his forehead with the back of his wrist, slaps the dust off his trousers.

"It's not there."

"What does that mean?"

"It means the deeds are in storage. Somebody has to go through the chain of title and find each transfer."

We're in a stalemate, he and I. The dress has expended its capital. I have no folded bills to bribe him with. There is a procedure, without a doubt. But I know about bureaucracies. He can make it happen fast, or see that it's lost in the backlog.

The old lady clears her throat. The clerk slaps a pad of post-its on the counter in front of me. "Name and address," he says. "I'll mail it to you." That's all. He doesn't even look up for me to thank him. He's hunched over the counter listening to the old lady. I want to stay a moment and try to parse her leaden accent. But I'm late.

Back at the office, I can't keep my curiosity out of my work. I make mistakes. I correct them. This goes on until I hear the bags being packed and the drawers shutting in the open area outside my office. I leave with the crowd.

I rise from the subway and walk home through the park. The men lean against the fences like they own them. They leer as I pass by, scanning my body and hissing, "God bless you, baby," as if their holy invocations made it all okay, as if it wasn't just another come-on.

Those hisses cling to my body, a layer of toxic dust. I go through the door to my apartment, bend to remove my heels, and sprint up to the third floor. The landing here is all mine. I unwrap myself from the dress and let it drop to the floor. I slide my underwear off with one hand and unlock the door with the other, shut it on the sullied clothes and step into the shower. When I come out, I put on a robe and ease into an armchair near the front of the apartment. A woman in a window across the street is cleaning house in her underwear.

My lover calls. I let it ring.

I sleep and I dream of the man in the picture. He came to me unbidden and now he is mine. He is nameless. A handsome man, a brilliant sky, a winning smile, his only story a dirty envelope and missed message. Once upon a time he had something a man called Cinco wanted. Money. A stolen thing. A thing that wants stealing. Or not a thing at all. Something intangible. A name. A code. A secret.

In my dream he is tall, and his voice is low and smooth as dark water. In my dream he doesn't see me. I follow him, stand close on a crowded train. I shadow him, invisible, just a stirring of the air that shudders through him from time to time. The place where he lives is nearly empty, white walls, an iron bed that could have been taken from an old sanitarium, a floor lamp, and a book whose name I cannot read. There is no ceiling, no roof, only the cloudless sky to shelter him. I lie down next to him on the bed and listen to his breath slip into sleep. As he begins to dream, I wake in tears.

If I found him now he would no longer be that man at all. Grown old, he would be twice my age, the winning smile would have carved lines around his mouth and eyes. The hair gone grey. The bright eyes might be all that remains. It weighs me down, this illusion of loss.

What I want, or what I believe I want, is to settle the matter, close it like a folder around a closed case. I want to fill in the blanks. I want to find out what went wrong.

In the morning before work, I walk through the neighborhood with one of my cameras. It's my oldest. The lens is yellowed and fogged. I take pictures of the weeds overtaking disused buildings and lots, bursting through a doorway or out the window of a rusted car to find the sun. I end up on the little street again, looking through the chain links of the fence thinking there might be something more to discover there. I hear a shuffle of gravel on pavement. Behind me, on a bench outside the warehouse, is a man smoking a cigarette. He's sprawled out, embracing the bench with his long arms like stretched wings. Maybe he's been there all along. The neighborhood is full of questions now. I'm searching the eyes of every man I see. This one nods at me, says nothing.

"You work here?" I ask.

"Yeah."

"Been here a while?"

He folds his arms back into himself and stubs out the cigarette. "Is this a job interview?"

"I just wondered what used to be there," I say, pointing to the vacant lot.

"Shit if I know," he says, and shuffles back into the warehouse.

The sun shines over the rooftops. I'm already late for work. I stuff the camera in my bag and head for the subway. I have learned nothing.

The train is tense again this morning. There's a man sitting near the doors. He is handsome and his clothes smell like money, but something is wrong. His eyes are stunned wide open, he never blinks. He has a slight smile that hints at severed neural pathways, inert violence. He wears a woolen hat on a warm morning. He speaks to the backs of the Japanese girls standing near him, "You're not listening," he says, over and over, varying his inflection a little with each repetition.

After work there is Jimmy. He turns up with flowers, pints of ice cream and his wanting eyes. The things he brings me are not the things I want. What I want are bits of detritus, raw flesh torn from the inside of him, indulgences I can't ask for. Things you are given are things that can be lost.

Tonight the wanting eyes are shocked with wonder when we fuck. I wake up to find he's been watching me sleep. I run my finger up his cheekbone. He will mistake this for something it's not.

—

A secret isn't really a secret until someone knows it's there. I go back to the library's reference room. The librarian with the grey ponytail looks up when the door clicks shut behind me. She adjusts the candy bracelets around her wrist and beckons me to hurry to the desk. "Well?" is all she says.

There's no one in the room but us, and still I whisper. "Did you ever break a law?"

She taps knuckle on the counter, thinking. "Traffic, yes."

"Everybody breaks traffic laws."

"I've broken some others," she tells me. "Now it's your turn."

I withdraw the envelope from my bag and lay it on the counter, with the steamed-open flap face up.

She runs a finger along the stiff, warped edge. She unfolds it and pulls out the picture, then turns it over. She's nodding. She looks at the address. "So that's not your house."

"No. And it's an empty lot now."

"What do you want to know?"

"Everything."

"Let's start with when. I can help you with that." She points to the partly illegible cancellation mark on the envelope, a bust portrait. "See this? That's Susan B. Anthony. Those dollar coins with her on them were released in December, 1978, and the post office used this cancellation mark for that month in her honor." She's smirking, prideful. I like her all the more for being pleased with herself.

"What don't you know about?"

She looks contrite, the way a schoolchild might: falsely. "Antiques," she says. "U.N. resolutions. Olympic medalists, other than the obvious. Patent law. Naval history, marine biology. The sea escapes me." She pushes the envelope across the counter to me. "What are you going to do with it?"

"I requested the records of who owned the lot, the house when it was a house."

"That's a lot of work for someone."

"I know."

"You're shameless, aren't you."

It's my turn for contrition. "Yes," I tell her.

"What do you want with him?" She points at the envelope. "The man in the picture."

It's the right question, and also the one that I haven't asked myself. She takes my silence for what it is.

"You don't even know, do you."

"I'm not sure yet," I say.

She begins to talk, taking the question of my motivation as a she would take a historical interpretation, a matter of insight and deduction. "You like knowing how to find things out."

I nod.

"But that's just what drew you in, I think. Now it's got all your attention, it distracts you the way a fresh affair might. Am I right so far?"

"Yes, I didn't realize until you said it, but yes."

"Is this your way, to fixate on things?"

"Not really."

She thinks a moment. "We are all so blind to ourselves," she says, sinking her chin into her hands propped on the counter. "Smart, but really just animals. Reflexes, responses, conditioning."

It's excruciating, listening to this, and I want to turn and leave. But her face is full of kindness, and she has more to say.

"Obsession is a kind of medicine, isn't it?"

I can feel tears coming, a block in my throat. "Thanks," is all I can say, and I put the letter back in my bag.

"The statute of limitations on mail tampering is only five years," she says, a legalistic consolation. "I hope you find him."

Her face looks broken, she's been too blunt. It must be one of her bad habits.

—

A day goes by. Subway, work, subway. The streets are quiet, the patterns are clear. It's been a while since I thought I saw my brother's shadow. I wonder what would be worse: to be found, or to know he never thought to look.

My lover calls. I let it ring.

One morning at the café, the coffee kid asks me what kind of jeans I like to see on a man. I'm not sure how to answer. I ask, "What are my options?"

Then a tall, narrow man with red stubble comes in. He pulls off his hat and orders a coffee. The kid hands him a cup and turns back to me. The man takes a sip and lets out a loud, unselfconscious sigh. His eyes are closed with satisfaction.

"Hey, I like to hear that, man," says the kid. "Makes me feel like I made the coffee right."

The tall man, he must be a regular, says, "Yeah, you're good. The quality is a little more stochastic on the weekends."

The kid looks confused. "I mean it's more variable," the man explains.

"Are you a math nerd?" I ask. The kid laughs, "Oh yeah, variables!"

I turn to the tall man, "No, I mean stochastic." The tips of his ears go pink and he looks at the floor. Sheepish, caught showing off.

"Oh," he says. "I'm a scientist."

They are a catalog of come-ons, these two, each a braggart in his own way. I feel unexpected tenderness for them both, the one impervious and the other so easily crushed. Lacking menace, all they've really done is give me power over them.

I become fixated on what passes between men and women in the streets. For a week it's the only thing I see, these scenes of solicitation and refusal. At the grocery store, I catch the manager watching hungrily as the checkout girl bends down to pick up a dropped coin. He and I stare at each other a moment. I would like it to be okay for him to appreciate her, but it isn't, because he is the boss and you can tell by his face he uses that for what he can. Something, this or else the heat, leaves me nauseous.

Now I've got a bag of food hanging from each hand. On the corner there's a beefy guy with a shaved head and gold chains. He's got sharp clothes and I've never seen him before. He says to me, "Hey beautiful, *tell* me those bags are heavy so I can carry them for you."

"Oh, they're not that heavy," I say, but I'm smiling, it's an easy day in the neighborhood, everybody spilling outside with the heat finally gone.

"My head is heavy cause I'm sad you said that." He's got his hand on his pleading heart, his forehead down.

Then a curvy woman crosses between us and says, "You head heavy because it's *big*."

Near the office, an expensive parking lot has a sign with pictures of employees who've worked there for 10, 20, and 30 years. I'm trying to imagine what that's like, when one of them gets out of a Range Rover and winks at me. I nod toward the sign. "Which one are you?

He points to a photo at the top of the sign. "Thirty years, baby."

"All that time," I say.

"I like cars," he shrugs. "And I get a no-show every other Friday."

"A no-show. How do I get one of those?"

"Stick around, baby. Stick around."

I can't quite parse the innuendo but it's there in the low roll of his voice all the same.

It's always this way. The men in the street call out to me. Always the same things, repeating themselves, a little bored, expecting no answer: "You want a date, baby?" and "Can I get your number?" and "You look fine." Others are singsong and earnest, "You look mad exotic," one tells me, "Put those legs away," another calls out, fingering his wedding ring, looking pained. They always ask, "You got a boyfriend?" and I always tell them yes.

It's always this way but today the air is thick with it. The bodega clerk tells me in a low voice how beautiful I am. Now I think: how would this work? The approach is plain, I am not in doubt of what they want. But how, what words exactly would we speak, how could one of these exchanges of street intimacy proceed? Maybe they know that, maybe it's that boundary of impossibility that gives them license to sing out their lust openly. Or, maybe not.

On Sunday I think about asking Jimmy. He's sitting on my fire escape. He's brought over a guitar to charm me with. He sings an old ballad and watches me while I get dressed on the other side of the window. He sings a little off key. As the song winds down, I decide not to ask. He comes from a warmer place, in terms of temperature and in terms of hearts, and I've already learned he doesn't like the way desire becomes profligate in the open spaces here.

The next morning, as I reach the entrance to the subway, the fat man puts down his begging cup and says, "Baby, you look good to-day," stretching each word to the limit of its strength.

5.

NATALIE'S PHOTOGRAPHS ARE BEAUTIFUL on purpose, not like the ones I make with my plastic lenses, where beauty comes as a chance procedure. Tonight she stops by to show me some pictures she's taken nearby. "I don't understand it," she says, twisting the ends of her long yellow hair around two fingers as she tabs through the photos on her laptop. "They're all a little blurry. Like my lens was fogged. But it wasn't. It's clean."

"That happened last time too," I remind her. "These streets are furtive. They don't want to be seen clearly."

"You're weird," she says, turning back to the computer.

"I'm telling you, these streets have things to hide."

Natalie shakes her head. She thinks she is a realist, logical, and that this will lead her to what is true. I've tried to tell her, but she'll never believe how mystical the truth can be.

Now I take the photograph out of the drawer I've stored it in. I hold it up for her to see. "When?"

She reaches out to take it but I keep my grip. I don't want her to see the back. She retracts her hand, her brow wrinkles. She leans forward to look at it more closely.

"Mid to late '70s, I think."

"How can you tell?"

"Well, the edges are rounded, and the image quality is too lousy to be 35mm film. My guess is it's from a really small negative, 110 film. Kodak Instamatics used that, the pocket ones. They made them in the '70s, they were super popular. And there's the paper too, it's got a funny grain." What Natalie sees when she gives the world scrutiny is always a revelation to me. I can't see past the man's face. Natalie sees paper, geometry, history.

"Besides, that's what men looked like in the late '70s. Don't you see?"

I envy the precision of her knowledge. I toss the picture back in the drawer.

"Who is it?"

"I don't know, I found it in a junk store. I got curious. He reminds me of someone."

"There's something so perfect about a man you won't ever meet." Natalie says. "He can't make any mistakes." She thinks I've fallen in love. I don't contradict her.

After she leaves, I go out for a walk. I want to check on the little street, but it fronts the road where the whores walk. I head the other way, and when I see the guy who's always got his arm in a sling, what I think is how easily people come and go here. How the neighborhood fills the blanks people leave behind, and opens spaces for them when they return. I haven't been here so long, but I've already seen it happen.

The man with the sling says "Hello, lady." It's what he always says. I know him and I don't know him. When I moved here, he and his cousin used to sit in lawn chairs in front of the parking lot, nodding out. They were lean and wolfish, even all slack in the creaking chairs. They were kind to me, protective when I passed by them on my way home late at night.

They both went away and only one came back: bowed, broken, swollen and aged. He is of the corner but he doesn't work there. He's had his arm in that sling for a year now, and the other day I saw him pushing a roll of bills inside it, but he doesn't have the sharp eyes of a lookout or the quick hands of a dealer's boy, and he's too old to be either. He's fucked up too often to be part of the trade. But still, just like Dealer a few blocks away, he works the crowd on the corner and across the street in the courtyard of the projects like a politician.

He asks me things when I pass by. How's my day, or where I'm going when I set off past the confines of his turf. There are things I want to ask him. Things like: what happened when you were gone that year, where is your cousin, what were you like before all this, why are you alone among the corner's players such a gentleman, wanting nothing from me but a warm smile. There are things I want to ask him but I never do. There is some unspoken contract it would break. We're neighbors. There are things it's better not to know.

—

Saturdays move slow in the neighborhood, but I'm impatient. I'm waiting for the mail. I try examining the trees. They're turning, and the lazy dawn rain has deepened their colors. The ivy is red, the molting sycamores reveal patches of green and yellow skin beneath damp grey bark. Across the street, my neighbor is standing idly in front of his small blue townhouse. He's the mayor of the block, a white man with an overgrown mustache. He's been here for thirty years, he told me once, moved here back when it was different. By different, he meant dangerous. Now he's retired, and he's always out in front sitting on the little bench by the door with his newspaper, pacing around the sidewalk barefooted, carrying a coffee mug whose steam is long spent. It's just a prop, signifying his mastery here, how the street is an extension of the house he owns. He can carry his dishes out here, and he needs wear no shoes. He knows all our names, and which cars belong to whom. He knows what's happening to the parking lot they're digging up at the end of the street. If I asked him, he might know about the vacant lot on the little street. But I don't ask him about that yet.

I sit down on my stoop, and catch his eye, patting the spot next to me. I've brought my coffee out too. A challenge. He comes over and stands by the iron gate, a few yards away. He's no fool, he knows I want something.

"Who lived here when you first moved in?"

"In your house, let me see."

"No, in general, in the neighborhood."

"Poor people. People who could afford to get out of the projects, but not that far, or didn't want to be far from the rest of their families."

"And you. You lived here too."

"There was one other white family, on the next block. They didn't last."

"What happened?"

"They never really got comfortable."

"With what?'

"With living here. With being the only white people in a poor black neighborhood. Barring your doors without looking like you're scared." He scuffs his flip flop against the edge of the gate, and then the words he utters startle me. "Aren't you ever scared?"

Honesty would serve me here, he's the only person who really knows the block and isn't strung into the illicit dealings of the corners. If I opened myself, he might tell me something I could use. "I don't think about it," I tell him. It's the best I can do.

I stroll down to the café, there's a long line. A young girl is off in the corner, dancing. Her moves are slow and subtle, cleaving to the bassline and the places where it stretches out a beat too long. She's unaware of anyone's eyes on her. Her face is awkward, but it's evident that she will grow up hard to resist. Her twin sister comes out of the bathroom. She's stiff and unmoved by the music. But she's taller, and there's more symmetry in her face. She will have to fashion herself aloof and unreachable to match her sister's charms. She leads the way out the door, and her sister shimmies along behind her.

When I get back home, it's there. At the top of the pile of mail inside the front door. A plain white envelope, City Hall postmark. It's a handwritten list of six names, each with a date of sale. They go back to the 1940s. There's a checkmark by one of them, 1980. I'm guessing that's when it was sold as a vacant lot. I imagine myself at the end of the story, that I will go back and tell it to the clerk, that he will be charmed for his part in the unfolding of it. But I know that I won't. I stare at the list. Line them up, I think. Knock them down. There is Cinco, the man the letter was sent to. And there is the young man in the photograph. There is some unofficial chain of title that will lead me to both of them.

I take my laptop out on the fire escape and watch the street wax and wane. The corner boys are hovering under the birch tree, shuffling in place, hoods up against the rain. "Man," one says. "It's *day*time. What we gonna do now?"

I see hundreds of people every day, some strange, some familiar, and the ones that fall in between. If I took a different subway line and saw you sitting in the corner, diligently shining your shoes, what's to say I would ever see you again. We cross paths and have no effect, just the ripple of awareness. Fleeting, unmemorable. Your name could have been Vasquez or Jones or Negri or Madder or Janicki or Flood. These are the six I've been given. I could have seen you. You on the corner, shining your shoes. What if it was you?

The story the deeds tell goes like this. Thaddius P. Jones bought it in 1947 and sold it to Enrico Negri in 1954. Another Negri, likely the son, sold it to Milos Janicki in 1971. Janicki seems to have died without a will, and the city sold the house to Josédalgo R. Vasquez in 1979, who sold it to Edward Madder in 1980. When Madder sold it to William W. Flood in 1985, it was listed only as a lot. No house. Flood defaulted last year.

Natalie's day job benefits me now. I call her and demand her passwords for the research database. She asks why and isn't surprised when I won't tell her. She surrenders anyway. I log in. This is what private detectives use too. I search for each man. It's thrilling and easy.

Three men named Josédalgo R. Vasquez are roughly the right age, have lived in the city for long enough, and are still alive. There are two named Flood of the right age. I write down what the database lists as their current addresses and phone numbers. I look for Madder; he is unaccounted for.

The sun has come back around the trees, sinking down, just a blur of light in the hazy clouds. I'm late to meet Jimmy is what the sun tells me. I close up the house and walk down the block.

I haven't seen anyone on Dealer's corner in a while. Tonight some of his boys are leaning on the bodega dumpster, aimless and slack.

So, I try something new. I talk to them. "Haven't seen your boss in a while, he ok?"

The fattest one steps forward and squints at me. "What boss?"

"That guy who's usually around. Older than you. Always says hello."

He shakes his head. It's like a teacher does, you'll get it someday honey, I know you will. "Lady, I know you ain't police," he says, and points his finger at his chest. "But to me, you might as well be."

—

Jimmy takes me dancing, and laughs when I skip a little on the way home. He stops for cigarettes and I keep on walking around the corner looking up at the moon. It's as big and bright as possible given the orbits and angles of planetary motion. It hangs low by the borough's lone skyscraper, dwarfing the neon clock on the tower. I stop a while, leaning on a parking sign's metal post, washed over by the impossibly lovely light. This man walks along, gnawing on a fried chicken leg, giving his back to the sky's spectacle. I stop him. "Did you see the moon?" I ask. He pulls the chicken away from his teeth and looks at me as if to say, but you don't *look* crazy, honey, what's up with that? Finally he plays along and asks, "It full?" I say, "Yeah, and it's really really big," and I point behind me. He shifts around a moment to see. Then he turns back to the way he'd been going, shakes his head, and sucks a sliver of meat from its bone.

I wait on the stoop for Jimmy. To my great surprise, he doesn't care about the moon either.

The night is quiet and it's quiet between us too. In the morning, I wake very early, and leave Jimmy a note, knowing it's not enough to patch the crumbling heart he'll feel in the interval between finding me missing and finding my words. Outside, I pace around the block, plotting my attack. The warm air is full of dew. The laundromat is empty, and almost elegant now that it is stripped of bright fabrics and plastic bottles and bored women. Only the man who runs it is there, passing a load of whites from a metal cart into a dryer. There's a radio on, in Chinese. The man comes over to weigh my bag. Then the radio switches to English, but it's not a radio after all, it's a language lesson. "When-will-the-car-be-ready?" The soothing voice asks three times, each with a different inflection. Then another round, Chinese and back to English: "I-am-ready-to-face-tomorrow."

I sit on the bench outside, listening to the lesson go on for a while, marking time until it's late enough to start knocking on doors. Finally I head for the subway.

There's no train, and there's no train. Everyone paces in small circles, or rocks back and forth on their feet. They lean out past the edge to check for lights, it's like a Busby Berkeley number, bodies fanning in sequence. There's a young woman dressed not like a secretary, but how she imagines a secretary would dress. It's a little too fanciful, her shoes are dainty and the headband holding back her dark hair is almost a tiara.

A skinny man swings a book by his side, his fingers marking his distracted place.

People are still pacing and checking their watches. Ten minutes go by. A few more. Then suddenly we are in it together. The skinny man steps close and asks me if I heard any announcements. He thinks it might be better to give up and walk to the next station. I ask him what he's reading, he says it's dry but useful, and reads the title aloud to me in a mocking voice. Then he rocks forward to check the tracks again.

Behind us, a bald man in dorky sneakers asks the girl where she got her tiara.

I nearly fall asleep as I ride the train to its farthest reach. Vasquez number one lives in a high-rise out here. I find his name and buzzer in the puzzling grid of metal buttons on the wall of the entrance. I am brazen. When the intercom crackles on, I say, "I'm from the Zoning Department." The door clicks. I go up.

An old, tired man stands outside his door at the end of the 10th floor hallway. "You're from where?"

"Zoning. We're sorting out some confusion on a deed. There's a property in question, at, just a moment." I pull out the narrow reporter's notepad from the bottom of my purse and flip through the pages. I tell him the address of the empty lot on the little street. "Are you the Vasquez who sold the property in 1980?"

"No lady, I never owned a thing in my life. That it?"

"That's that, yes. Thank you." I turn back to the elevator.

"Hey lady," he calls out after me. "You city people got no phone? They workin' you Sundays?" The smile on his face is not friendly. "Maybe you want a better story than that."

I have a better plan for the next one. The address for this Vasquez is in a modest neighborhood of detached houses. I walk up and down the block. I mime confusion. From the house next door emerges a woman whose rolling fat undulates as she walks. "No time for you Witnesses today," she says, shaking her hand, no, no, no.

"Oh, no," I say. "I'm just looking for a house."

"Nobody selling on this block."

"No, I'm not buying. I'm looking for where my mother lived when she was little. She showed me a picture. But I only know it's on this street, near the subway." I scratch the pavement with the toe of my shoe. I want her to think my mother is dead. I want her sympathy. I want to slip her suspicions.

"Tell me what the house looks like, maybe I can help."

"Kind of like that one," I point to the Vasquez house. "How long have they lived there?"

"That house, they've been there since the grandpa bought it, one of those soldier loans back when."

"Oh, that can't be it then." I'm about to turn away when I realize I'm walking away from the scene without a crucial detail. Who owns a place is not always who lives there. "But I remember my mother talking about them, I think. They owned some apartments somewhere else. The mom was always griping about the tenants."

She looks puzzled. "No, that must be some other family. Look around you," she waves a hand at the street. "People here are just getting by." She stands a moment, watching me. Now I feel like I can't leave until she goes on her way. "You got a real needle in the haystack project there, don't you."

Yes, I tell her, and she walks on, shaking her head.

Vasquez number three lives back in my own neighborhood, the Italian section down by the highway. At the end of my block, a cop is walking her beat, seeing nothing, sending text messages as she strolls. The corner boys, unexpectedly, are harmonizing on someone's stoop. Near the junior high school, a little kid is trying skateboard tricks on the stairs. He keeps falling down. The big kid says, "it's okay, skateboarders are allowed to hang on to something," and then he winks at me.

The house is a four-story brownstone with generous windows. An iron gate encloses the front yard, whose most prominent feature is a faded St. Lucy statue in a plexiglass shrine. Across the street a man is hosing down his sidewalk, eyeing me casually. I think about waiting until he's done, but it's clear there are eyes on this street, whether I can see them or not. I take out my reporter's notebook and open the iron gate. As it creaks, I can feel the man's gaze heavy on my back.

There are two bells. The top one says "Rosetti." The bottom one says "Vasquez." The ground floor apartment is dark, the windows covered only by yellowed shades. The three floors above have matching curtains. What I've learned is he's got a ground floor apartment, and he isn't home. I hear rustling and look up. There's an old woman looking out one of the parlor floor windows. She taps on the screen. "You need him?"

There's some construction scraps stacked by the trash bins. I take a wild stab. "I need some work done on my place. Someone from my office recommended him."

She cackles a little, tosses her old grey head back. "You don't want my brother for that honey."

I'm not sure if she means she doesn't buy it, or she advises against it. I just thank her and go back out onto the street. From the gate, I turn back. She's still there. "It's such a pretty neighborhood here. My sister's looking for an apartment. Do you know anybody needing a tenant?"

"You want my brother after all, then." She points down the street. "He owns two of them."

"But he lives in yours?"

"I cook," she shrugs, as though that were an obvious explanation. "I cook Spanish. He likes it better than my husband does. My husband eats at his mother's. I want nothing to do with those noodles she makes. Send your sister by on Friday, he'll be around then."

"Thanks," I wave, a bright smile.

Walking back home, I see what a trap my improvisation has made for me. Now I need a sister. I'm assessing my options. I can skip work and go back pretending to be my own twin. I can rope Natalie into this, but she'll want to know why and I don't want to tell her. I'm hoarding it. I'm a miser of secrets. And besides, I own a wig.

On the wide avenue, three men with flags are leading a parade of old ladies clutching lilies and a motley brass band sweating a dirge from their horns. They trail along behind a statue of Jesus on the back of a pickup truck. I ask one of the old ladies, she waves a hand encircling the scene and says, "It's holy."

Up in my kitchen, I stand by the back window and look at my notebook, the list of names and addresses. The men named Flood will have to wait until next weekend. There's one more thing I want to do tonight. I call Jimmy and tell him to come over at 10. "Bring a bolt cutter," I tell him. "A big one."

An afternoon haze overtakes me. I run down to the bodega for coffee. The old dude with the beatnik beard is strolling around like he owns the place. The corner boys let it ride.

In front of the bodega, that guy who wanted to carry my groceries is back. He's not looking so fine today, a grubby t-shirt and sweat beading up on the dome of his head. He's pacing off some anger, punching the air. "He's not even a citizen. What's he talking about," he grumbles to the guys by the bodega. He spits in the gutter. "Cocksucker."

Back toward home, there's a young woman, she's small and her clothes are smaller. Her face is shadowed by a stiff trucker's hat. Beside her is a beanpole of a man rocking a baby carriage back and forth. He's older, and just shy of homely. "Excuse me," the man says, as he points a finger back and forth between him and the girl. "If you saw the two of us together, would you think we made a fine couple?" The girl is giggling, hiding her face further under the hat.

"You're both beautiful," I say.

"See," he says to the girl, and then turns back to me. "She don't want to be with me. What's that about?"

"I guess that's her problem, right?" I say, catching the girl's eye so that we are in on the joke together.

I walk on by and the man calls out after me. I look back and there he is, all gangly with a silly grin and a big thumbs-up.

The coffee propels me through the night. Now it's almost ten. I put on my darkest jeans, a black hoodie. I bring a camera, my excuse for the expedition. Jimmy is never late. When the doorbell rings, I grab a tiny flashlight and go down to meet him. He's standing there on the stoop with the giant, long handled claw.

"Where's your bike?"

"My bike?"

He holds up the bolt cutters. "I thought you lost your key."

"No. Come with me." I tug his arm and lead him down the street.

We walk by one of the whores, swaying on her candy red heels, and another, more desperate, with pockmarked skin and runs in her stockings. Candy Shoes nods at the bolt cutters, "Y'all got a license for those?" She cackles softly and keeps swinging her hips as a truck crawls past with its tinted window rolled down to look a her.

"What's going on?"

"We're going exploring," I tell him. The fact is he will do what I ask him to. I stop at the corner of the little street. All the lights are out in the two houses. We walk past them to the fence gate.

I point to the chain. "That. Cut that." He does. I swing the gate open, Jimmy follows me in.

He kicks an empty beer bottle, it grates on the blacktop. "Shh," I say. "We're not supposed to be in here."

He leans back against the fence. He's stewing. I can feel it. I set the camera down on the ground pointed toward a shock of broken glass in the grassy ledge between the lot and the canal. I fuss with the settings so it will keep the shutter open for five minutes, exposing the film to what little flecks of light there are. Jimmy watches me kneel over the camera. "You could have just told me it was for that."

"You like surprises," I say, even though it isn't true. I'm the one who likes surprises. "Let's look around."

"We might get in the picture."

"It's ok, we'll just be ghosts." I start pacing the boundary of the lot, along the fence. I'm looking in the space where the blacktop ends just short of the fence. It's full of weeds, some of them on their way to being trees, their leaves grown massive to collect the light their stalks need to grow thick and tall. It's what you'd expect. Broken glass, sundry trash, a fallen tree branch angled near the corner. I hear the shutter click, and walk over to wind the film and take another.

Jimmy is poking his foot around in a thicker patch of weeds on the other side of the lot. "Anything interesting over there?"

"Nope. How long are we going to be here?"

"Not too long. I'm sorry, I thought this would be a little more exciting. Breaking and entering!"

"I'm glad you didn't do it alone."

I'm still walking the fence. At the back corner I hear something rustling in the weeds and skitter away. I find a fallen branch and rattle it through the weeds to be sure. The branch stops short of the fence. There's something solid there. I look back at Jimmy, he's got his fingers wrapped in the fence, looking out over the canal. I shine the tiny flashlight on the weeds, take a deep breath, and bend the plants aside with one hand. It's a pile of singed aluminum siding, dented and blackened.

All the sudden, Jimmy's behind me. "Stand still," he says. "There's someone in the street." I like it when the man in him comes out. He holds my shoulders. There are two voices, a bottle breaks, another flies into the canal. They are men. They are laughing. They are drunk. Their sneakers squeak on the street as one calls a race and the other springs into action. They're gone.

I show Jimmy the charred fragment of siding. "What do you think?"

"Looks like there was a fire. Something burned, that's for sure. Was there a house here?"

"I don't know."

"Does it matter?"

"No, I'm just curious."

"You're always curious."

Being known is what most people want, but it makes me want to run. I change the subject. I take Jimmy home with me. He deserves it.

On the way to work the next morning, I'm daydreaming, imagining the missing house on the little street in flames. A man catches my eye. He's standing by the doors as we cross over the bridge in the morning's clear light. He's wiry and unshaven. He looks at me just a beat too long. Then his gaze drifts back to his girlfriend, her back is to me. She tugs a hank of her long dark hair. He shrugs, and raises a flat hand to the level of her chin. He wants to change her. She shakes her head. They've been holding hands but now he drops hers and turns back to the view of the wide river. She keeps looking at him as he rests his temple on the glass and watches the blue girders of the bridge flash by. She puts her fingers on his chest, and getting no response she settles back. He looks at me again, his eyes say: it would be different if it was you. But he is wrong. Who among us is happy?

When I get to Midtown, I ride up in an elevator full of women talking about their insomnia. I've seen them before, they go out and smoke at 10:30 every day, and I always wonder if they're on a punch clock or just accustomed to the rhythm. They fill the elevator with the scent of soured smoke. As I leave the elevator, I can't help sniffing my sleeves to see if it has clung to me. It hasn't. I close the door to my office and call Natalie at the newspaper. "How do I find out when a house burned down and why?"

"God, I have no idea."

"Ask someone. One of those boys on the city desk. They'd do anything for you, wouldn't they?"

"I'll call you back."

My in-box is empty. That won't last long. I go outside to the corporate piazza where people go to smoke. At a table, a girl on a cellphone is droning vapid relationship advice. All around her, everyone is kissing. As is often the case, I feel for just a moment like I'm dreaming. I sit down on a stone bench and turn my face up to the sun. After a while, I imagine that I can hear papers rustling on my desk. I go back up, there's a contract to proof. I want to think I have special powers of perception, that I did hear the papers. What I really heard was the sound of probability.

Natalie doesn't call back until the end of the day, but she's got an answer. The Fire Department has a records archive. She gives me the number. "Say you're me," she says. "Say it's for the paper." I try calling but they're closed already. City bureaucrats keep bankers' hours.

Back in the neighborhood, things are jumping. Dealer's back. I haven't seen him for a while. He's glad-handing his corner boys as I cross the street. He looks good, better-kept than he used to. "How you feelin' baby," he sings out to me through a big grin, "long time no see." He says it just right, familiar and curious, as if I were the one who'd been gone all that time.

Later, Natalie stops by. We go up to the roof with a bottle of wine and settle into the lawn chairs I keep up there. "So what's with the fire?"

"Just an empty lot. Somebody said there used to be a house. I get the feeling there's a story. So I want to find out. Why."

"What kind of story?"

"You know, just a neighborhood story."

"Is this about that picture you showed me?"

I nod. I can give her that much.

Natalie pours herself some more wine and points to the building across the street. It's one floor taller, and from the darkness we can see a couple making out on the top-floor fire escape. He keeps pushing into her, she's bumping her head on the bars, adjusting. "What do you do with it all?"

"All what?"

"All the stories."

"I write them down." It's a lie, but it gives some sense to my fixations.

—

Walking through the projects toward the subway, I see two beat up cars and a van parked on the courtyard sidewalk next to one of the towers. Maybe a dozen men are standing around by the van, it all seems friendly enough. But there are small groups of people clustered around the courtyard, watching, keeping their distance. I get closer and I see what it is, an undercover in a football jersey is jangling two pairs of cuffs on his finger.

On the far side of the trouble, I walk past a man in a neatly tucked t-shirt. He's talking to an old lady with a granny cart. "I didn't know they sell drugs in that building."

"Shit yeah," the old lady says.

I get to work early, just in time for the bureaucratic day to begin. I call the Fire Department again. A woman answers in a monotone, "Fire Department Records can I help you," as if it were all one word.

"I'm trying to find records about a fire at a particular property."

"Address and year please."

"I don't know the year exactly."

"Hold please."

It's a long time before the line picks up again. It's a man's voice this time. "Records," he says.

"Hi, I'm a reporter, I'm trying to get records about a fire."

"Charlotte said you don't know what year. That makes it difficult to find."

"I'm a reporter," I tell him, naming Natalie's newspaper. "I'm following up on a tip."

I hear him sigh. "I should ask you for a formal request in writing for something like this."

"I can send you one if you need me to." Brinksmanship.

"I'd have to do it anyway, wouldn't I. Do you have at least a vague idea of when?"

"Between 1980 and 1985."

"Okay, could be worse. What's the address?"

I give it to him. "What happens now?"

"Call me in a few days, I'll see what I can do."

Someone knocks on my door. It's the assistant with a pile of contracts. I hang up the phone and put on my glasses. I stare at the pages and wait for the errors to reveal themselves to me.

After work, I'm walking up the street toward home and I see a man standing in front of my house. He's looking back and forth from the basement apartment of my building to the one next door. He's maybe 45, in jeans and a bomber jacket, salt and pepper hair. He looks too suburban for this neighborhood. I can't put my finger on it, maybe his jeans have been ironed. He looks up at me, sheepish, and explains, "I'm looking for my sister's place. She just moved here with her husband. Latina girl? I can't remember which one is her house."

"Well," I say, pointing to my building. "It's not this one."

"Great," he says and stands in front of the house next door with his hands on his hips. He's not ready for the door yet. He paces a little as I walk up the stairs and then gathers himself. He walks through the iron gate. I hear it scraping on the sidewalk.

As I close the door behind me, I think: that man is an axe murderer.

I'm letting all this mystery get to me.

I toss through a sleepless morning, then linger over daybreak breakfast at the diner. The old people are dabbing the butter off their toast. The man in the suit speaks Italian in a heavy voice. The boy's face twitches as his father talks. They don't seem to know each other very well.

It's hot again after a few chill days. The kids on the subway are bursting out of themselves. A curvy girl in jeans and a skinny boy in school uniform trousers are sparring around the vertical pole, daring each other to take off articles of clothing, pretending that they might. She offers a seated boy a lap dance. He tentatively accepts, knowing there's a catch here somewhere. She laughs at him, "No way!"

"I bet you all choke your chickens every single night," she laughs again.

"What about you, huh?" ventures the boy she refused to dance for.

"Not me, no way. I'd never do that."

"Never say never," says the skinny boy.

"That one I'm sure. Never."

Then a boy who had been silent through all this says, "You're what, 16? Say you live to be 90. It's statistically impossible in all those years you'd never."

"Statistics is for white people," she spits back.

At work I call the archivist at the Fire Department again. "You got an interesting one here, seems to me," he tells me. "Two fires. The first one is 1981, house was vacant except for one old lady on the third floor, report says she'd lived there most of her life. She called it in. She got out and watched her worldly goods burn. The boys put it out, what was left was a bombed out shell. Enough structure that it could have been renovated."

"What was the cause?"

"That's the beginning of what's odd about it. Was electrical in nature, but the inspector found that the wiring had been tampered with. It's hard to prove anything in a situation like that, right? Bad repair work by the super maybe. No criminal charges."

"But there was another one."

"Yeah, 1984. That one was simpler. Owner left the building as it was. No renovations. He told the inspector he was saving his money to fix it up. *Gotta put the egg back in my nest egg.* That's what he said to the inspector. Very colorful."

"Was it the same inspector?"

"No, the first one had retired by then."

"Cause?"

"Arson, open and shut. Gasoline fire, the pattern of the initial blaze consistent with an ignitable liquid pour."

"Who did it?"

"Nobody charged with it."

"Really?"

"It was a rough neighborhood back then. Let 'em burn each other down, I'd suspect that was the sentiment."

"Can I have the names of the inspectors?"

The line goes dead for a moment. I hear him breathe. "I'm not allowed to release that information."

"Even to a reporter?"

"Did you know that in the 1980s," he says, "There were only three fire inspector positions for the entire city, couple hundred thousand fires. Those men were busy. Just three of them. Every time you read about a fire in the paper, it was one of those three guys telling you about it. Budgets back then. The city was broke."

I am trying to figure out if there's some way to kiss him through the phone wires. The ways people divulge things without divulging them are myriad and marvelous.

"They always skimp in the wrong places don't they," I respond.

"That's right honey. Truer words never spoken. Can I do anything else for you? There's only one of me here, and I've got a pile of records to process."

"Thanks."

"Good luck with your article."

I hang up and dig through one of Natalie's databases. The fires on the little street weren't news, but other fires were. I get the names of the inspectors and run them through the identity database. Two are dead, the last has moved south. I get his number from information and place the call. He sounds a little groggy when he answers the phone.

"Hi, I'm sorry to trouble you. I'm a writer in the city and I'm working on an article about the history of my neighborhood."

"I'm left there years ago, lady."

"Yes, but you were a fire inspector in the '80s, isn't that right?"

"Sure."

"Well there's a particular fire that some folks have mentioned to me. Unsolved arson, a little building by the canal."

"I worked about six thousand cases in the '80s, and there were two other guys did the same."

"So you wouldn't remember this one, I guess." He's gruff and surly, but I think I hear a particular edge in his voice. What it is that I hear is pride. I take a chance. "And I suppose at your age, the details are slipping away, aren't they. I'm sorry to bother you."

He bites. "Hang on there. I got the mind of an elephant. Old, my ass. Where was it?"

I tell him the address, the previous fire.

"I remember that one. You know why? Because that one really pissed me off."

"How so? It was vacant. Nobody got hurt, I thought."

"When nobody gets hurt, there's one thing that still really burns me. I knew who the perp was. I had two eyewitnesses. Respectable folks."

"But you didn't give it to the police?"

"The police didn't want it."

"What do you mean?"

"The narcs wanted the perp more than I did. They ran the show back then. Stuck-up fuckers. Pardon me. The language."

"I've heard worse. Thanks a lot for your time."

"Jesus, I gotta go take some antacids now. Ulcer doesn't like the past. Nice talking to you," he says and hangs up.

After work I stop at the lab to pick up the photographs from the night in the empty lot with Jimmy. They're dark, underexposed, all but the streetlamp's pool of light on the canal, the light itself fragmented into lines, the water's oily surface blurred with soft motion. In the best one, there's a smudge in the penumbra of the light, that's Jimmy, leaning on the fence. The camera had been just a hasty excuse for the trespass, but now I like that there's murky evidence of it. That evening happened. This is all happening. There is my obsession, there is my canal, there is the man I keep in the shadows. At home, I tack it to the wall in the area dominated by cement and darkness. I wonder when Jimmy will notice it. If he'll see himself there at the edge of things.

In the morning, I wake to the siren's call, growing louder as I come out of sleep. There are fire engines roaring around the projects pretty regularly, and for the most part I tune them out, along with the beeping backup warnings of the garbage trucks and the shrieking laughs of the teenage girls on the sidewalks. Tonight it's impossible not to see the trucks and their lights. In part it's because now I've got fires on my mind. Mostly though, it's the burning smell in the air.

I slip into yesterday's clothes and follow the charred scent. My neighbor down the street is watching from the sidewalk in front of his house. He was a fireman years ago. A fall through the roof retired him, he likes to say, and he limps from the hip on damp days. He's got a well-groomed afro and a gorgeous '70s Lincoln painted fire-engine red, of course.

"Somebody's going to work," he says.

There are people on any block who observe the comings and goings on the street, who keep its pulses. He is one of them, and at first I think he means me. Not that I am headed for my office, which I am. That he somehow knows about the quest I'm on.

"Me?" I ask, and instantly see my mistake.

"No, I mean over there," he says, pointing toward the trucks. He rocks back and forth on heels. "I miss it," he says. "You smell that and the adrenaline gets going."

Then he closes his eyes. "Smells like victory."

We're quiet for a long time, watching the smoke wash through the air. "I didn't see any flames."

"They're inside," he says. "Smoke coming out the windows. It's a little fire, looks to me. Just a lot of smoke. They'll make quick work of it."

"There must be a lot of fires around here."

"What makes you say that?"

I realize how it sounds. Like I mean black people cause fires, or poor people. "Old buildings, renters. The projects can't be too well built. I was thinking a lot of electrical stuff must go bad." But he was right. I meant that poor people might not care about their houses, or that there are so many people drunk and on drugs around here, falling asleep with lit cigarettes. I am guilty of thinking in stereotypes and I am also partially right and it makes me squirm under my coat.

"You're not wrong," he says, and I think by the look on his face that he means all of it, all of what I haven't said, too.

"Hey, how long have you lived around here?"

"My whole life."

I try as hard as I can to make this all seem incidental. "I was down by the canal the other day." I'm watching his face to see if it works. "There's a vacant lot on that little street. What happened to the house that was there?"

"I didn't know you were into real estate."

"Oh, no. I can't afford that. I'm just curious."

"Curious." He stops a moment. "Well, there was a big fire. Actually two of 'em. Somebody wanted that building torn down the cheap way."

"Did they figure it out?"

"Honestly I never paid much attention to the follow-up. We were busy. Fight a fire you have to be focused on the moment at hand. Always. I don't remember a lot from those years, other than my baby girl's smiles and the fires themselves."

"What do you remember about them?"

"How the heat moved, what collapsed first, who we pulled out, who we lost."

"You could write a book about that," I say. "All those stories, the stories of the fires. Of the flames and what they did."

He turns to me, grins. "Who says I'm not?"

—

The next night, I'm on the way home from a late dinner with Natalie when Dealer comes up behind me out of what seemed the empty darkness. "Hey pretty girl," he says. "How you feelin'?" His shaved head is shining in the moonlight.

"I'm good," I tell him. "You?"

He walks alongside me. He's a little too close. He could put his arm around me from where he is, and I'd just fit under the crook of his armpit. I can feel the heat of his body, the fabric of his jacket just a whisper away from mine. I don't like it at all.

"You know what, me, I'm fine as long as everything goes like it supposed to do."

"Yeah."

"Boys told me somebody messin' around in that empty lot few nights ago." He points to the little street.

I'm not sure how to play this. It's a warning, but I don't know how it's supposed to work. "That a fact?"

He stops and holds onto the meat of my arm. "Don't fuck around, you on thin ice here now. All the eyes on this street are mine."

I look into his. Their warm twinkle is gone. They are hard and dark as the tinted windows on his car.

"So you and your skinny boyfriend. What you doin' breaking into that lot?"

I pull my arm loose from his grip. "Thin ice? It's your lot? I'm sorry. I'll pay for the lock."

"Ain't no matter who holds the paper on it. What I wanna know is what you doin' there?"

"I was taking pictures." It's the truth. I have evidence.

"Taking pictures. In the middle of the night in a lot full of weeds and rats. You a funny one."

If I didn't feel so guilty, what would I say? I'd rattle on. "The light off the canal is pretty. I made some long exposures. You want to see?"

"How come you didn't take them from the end of the street. Canal just as pretty there."

I am sparring, a fleet footed bantamweight, I'm dancing around him, just a second ahead. "The light pole on the other side. I wanted it in the center. Symmetry."

He shakes his head. A little corner of a smile.

I've got him, I think. Pressure's off. "I poked around while I was waiting for the camera—it took a couple minutes each shot. Was there a house there before? It seemed like maybe there was a fire."

He stops me in my tracks. I look at him, I tip my head to the side, puzzled, innocent. "What's the big deal about the lot?"

"The big deal is it ain't none of your concern. You feel me?"

"Okay," I say. "I got it." I want him to get out of my way, but he stands there, it feels like forever, a wall between me and what I want to know, between me and the place where I am safe.

—

On Friday I call and say I'll be late, then I root through the mess in the hall closet until I find the wig. It's moppy and dishwater brown. When I found it at the discount wig store, I couldn't even believe they'd make a wig that color. Who would choose it? But I have, because what I want is to look plain. To become unmemorable. I tuck the loose strands of my scarlet hair beneath it and check the mirror. It's not bad. I'm sure the old lady described me simply. "Fake red hair like a teenager," or something like that. It can be useful, the striking hair. It's all anyone remembers. Without it, I fade into the background.

I hit the street. By the lot at the end of the street, there are four men, huddled around a walleyed dog, their backs to the sagging fence. They're always there. The accumulated stink of their cologne and their sweet cigarillos is unfathomable. Last week I saw a pigeon splattered in the street in front of them. It is still there.

I take the long way around, I'm steering clear of Dealer's corner. The last thing I need is for him to see me waltzing around in a wig.

I'm practicing lies all along the way, and when I get over to Vasquez's house, he's out front, raking the leaves around the St. Lucy. There's something awkward, hunched about his motions. I rattle the gate and call out "Hello." When he turns I see the source of the awkwardness. He's only got one arm.

I'd put him around sixty. Thin legs, barrel chest. He's wearing dirty workman's pants and a sweatshirt streaked with white paint. His hair is gray and buzzed like a soldier's. There's a gold watch around his wrist. I wonder how he gets it on. He doesn't say anything, so I do. "I'm looking for an apartment. Your sister said to ask you."

"Okay, hang on." He drops the rake and goes inside, after a while comes back out with a ring of keys. "This way," he says, and I follow him across the street and down to the far end of the block. He seems to be perfectly comfortable with me trailing behind him. No interest in small talk. He lets me in the front door of a brick apartment building, and I follow him up the stairs. On the third floor, at the end of the hall, he swings an unlocked door open and extends his arm across the threshold. "After you."

It's a nice place, well-kept. The door opens onto a big room with windows looking out into the fiery leaves of a tall tree. The paint is fresh, the floors are shiny with varnish.

He points to one end and then the other. "Kitchen, bedroom, bathroom over there."

I walk around, open doors, look pensively into the closets. I end up in the kitchen, leaning back against the counter. I'm imagining my grandmother's dime-store dishes stacked in the cabinets.

Vasquez is standing over by the windows. He narrows his eyes at me. "Look, lady, if you're from Code, you know you gotta come here with papers. I'm tired of you people on my ass."

I laugh, but I hear how nervous I sound. "I'm nobody, don't worry."

"Well, you don't want an apartment, I can tell you that much."

I set a hand on my hip and lean into it. There's a way through this, but cautious. "How do you know?"

"You didn't ask the questions. Heat included, is it noisy, stuff like that. People turn on the shower, flush the toilet."

"Well, maybe I just don't like the place."

He is treating this as hypothetical, and he's a little amused. He thinks a moment. "You'd look more awkward. You'd be trying to get out." He leans back on the wall, crosses one foot over the other. "So, what is it?"

"I'm wasting your time, I'm sorry."

"You gotta have a reason for this. So tell me, and then we're even. I can tell the boys down at the bar about the kooky chick who didn't want to rent an apartment."

"I'm writing something. A novel." I look down at my toes. The lies come to me like water, but my face can't always conceal them.

"So?"

"I've been looking at apartments, I'm trying to figure out where my main character lives."

"You're crazy. Don't you just make that stuff up?"

"Usually, but I got stuck. I couldn't see her at home. I couldn't figure it out, so I just started looking at places. I'm really sorry."

"So is this it, does she live here?"

He wants her to, I can work this. I shake my head. "No, it doesn't feel right."

"Oh."

He taps his foot. He's in no hurry to shuffle me out.

I take a risk. "What happened to your arm?"

"Tet happened to my arm."

"I'm sorry."

"Whatever. I lived. That's something." He's looking me hard in the eyes. I scuttle the urge to look away. "I got another building, but it's the same layout. You wanna see?"

"I think it's more dumpy than this. Gritty. She's a little desperate."

"I used to own a place down by the canal. Woulda been perfect for you, I bet. Gritty all right. Had a dive bar full of thugs on the ground floor."

"What happened to it?"

"It was a rental. Supposed to be easy money, but you know. Dodgy neighborhood. The blacks were up to all kinds of things. Somebody was dealing drugs outta there. Too many cops nosing around. My uncle made me sell it. He didn't want any attention on the family."

"Who bought it?"

"Just some guy, was a friend of my army buddy. Dead now, probably. Kind of a dirtbag."

We're both quiet a while. There's a whole room between us, but I feel like we're dancing a slow box step, he's holding the small of my back with his good hand, I've got mine on his lame shoulder.

"I bet you're not writing a book either, are you."

I look at my feet. "No."

"Tell me the truth this time, what's your story."

Maybe the truth will work, I think. "I'm trying to find someone."

"You lose someone?"

"Not exactly. I have something that belongs to someone else."

"What makes you think I'd know anything about it?"

"It's got something to do with that building you used to own. I knew about that. I knew you sold it to a man named Madder. I also know it burned down."

"That's just some old trouble over there. Ancient history. You should leave it lie."

"What kind of trouble?"

"The bad kind. A soap opera of trouble."

"I don't want any trouble, but I need to find someone," I say again, as if it carried the weight of logic.

"Lady, look for who you wanna look for, but that building is gone anyhow."

"Then why did you tell me in the first place?"

He's staring into my eyes again, unflinching. "Because you told all these lies to find out. And maybe it'll keep you safe to know it." He shrugs, turns away a little. "Plus it got you to stay a little longer. You're good to look at, you know that."

I want to buy him a drink, show up at his local bar and dazzle his drinking buddies. I want to take off the wig and show him how beautiful I am.

He pushes off the wall and heads for the door. As he's locking it behind us, he turns to me. "To my mind, the real question is why did you tell *me* all that stuff. You don't know a thing about me." He raises an eyebrow.

He's right.

OCTOBER

6.

JIMMY COOKS ME DINNER in my kitchen. I watch the precise motion of the knife in his hands, the hands that make music, that pluck vibrations in taut strings. My table is strewn with books and half-read newspapers. I refuse to move them away, I only push the piles toward the edge of the table, clearing just enough space for our plates. Jimmy puts his hands on his hips and laughs. He seems to understand that the domestic character of the evening doesn't rest easily on me. He seems not to mind my discomfort. He puts his beer down on a copy of *The Odyssey*. The meat in the oven sizzles.

"What do you do, at night. Other nights?" It's not a jealous question. His voice is easy, none of the knots of attempted detachment. I'm a curiosity to him, more and more. He's playing. He's trying to match the distance I keep.

I pretend not to know all that. I point at him with my fork, a mock defense. "Are you asking me if I sleep with other men?"

"Do you seriously think I'd ask you that? Wouldn't I snoop while you went to the bathroom or something, search for your journal or your box of photographs?"

"So you mean how do I live."

"Yes. How do you live the many hours of your life I don't know about."

It's a terrible, unanswerable question, but I can see it's asked honestly. I try to meet him there. "I spend a lot of time alone. I walk around the neighborhood, I talk to the people who talk to me. I take pictures, you know that."

"Why did you come here?"

"Next question." I can only turn one page at a time.

"Do you have friends? You never talk about any."

"Natalie," I tell him. "She's the first person I met when I moved here. She's my friend."

"Why did you need to move?"

It was the first thing I asked him, I recall, why did he come here, and he never asked in return. I was so cagey that day, he has been playing his cards well. I'm not sure how to talk about the act of leaving a loss behind. Not yet, not with this man. "My old city fell out of love with me," is what I say.

He shrugs at my retreat from specificity. He picks up his beer and wipes the damp ring off the book with his sleeve.

"How long until the food is done?"

"At least an hour, why?"

I stand up and take his hand. "Come on, come with me a minute."

He follows me, I knew he would. I lead him down the stairs to the street. We walk around the corner and the pavement glittering with shattered glass. Jimmy pulls back. He knows where we're going.

"What is it with you and the empty lot?"

I realize, though Jimmy does not know this, that it's the same question he's already asked. The one I can't answer. "I think something happened there, a long time ago. Didn't it feel spooky when we broke in?"

We're at the little street now. The lights are on in the house next to the lot. We stand on the corner for a few minutes, watching shadows pass behind the curtains in the front windows. "I don't know," Jimmy says. "It's just an empty lot."

"There was a fire there. I looked it up."

"There are lots of fires in this city."

The evening's charmed ease has worn off him. He's impatient now. "Let's go. I have to turn the meat." He starts back around the corner.

A curtain rustles. The door begins to creak open. The form of the man who steps outside is so familiar it doesn't matter that his face is still in the shadows. It's Dealer. A boy with a surgical mask around his neck pops his head out too, Dealer sends him back inside. So this is where Dealer's operations are. I don't know if he's seen us. I do the only thing I can do. I turn slowly and follow Jimmy back to my house.

After dinner Jimmy slips his fingers over my collarbone and slides my shirt away. He touches me gently, gently and then grabs a fistful of my hair and pulls me down on the bed. He's like that, Jimmy. Stronger than he looks.

I sleep. I dream of bicycles with flat tires and narrow escapes. I keep getting away just as the dream shifts, I'm somewhere else and then I'm running again. I can't see who chases me, but I feel the gravitational force of his approach. I feel him behind me and then I wake up gasping. Jimmy pulls me close and the warmth of him draws me back down into sleep.

In the morning I'm still shaken from the dreams. I feel I haven't slept at all. I pass by the man from the house next door, he looks away, as always he does. He's younger than he is old, and thin, and the thing about this man is the tremendous pouches under his eyes, sagging down to his sharp cheekbones. I imagine that he never sleeps. His landlady lives on the ground floor of his building, but it is him I see on the weekends tending to the things growing in barrels out front. Pulling weeds tenderly, pinching wilted flowers. I wonder if he has made peace with his insomnia. Maybe the pockets beneath his eyes are filled with undreamt dreams.

When I rise from underground in Midtown, there's a plain-faced couple lingering by the subway steps, they're pressed close and kissing softly. It's lovely to watch, it makes you want to kiss the next person who walks by. But no one else sees them. Everyone is late for work, or dazzled by the neon lights.

Connection or coincidence, I can't stop asking myself. The photograph, the fire, Dealer's cutting house. The layers and layers of vice. The papers on my desk are riddled with errors, and I am grateful, hunting them pushes everything else from my mind. I stay late. The assistant brings me another contract. I thank her and look back at the papers on my desk. I can feel her lingering in the doorway. I imagine the wobbling ankles, the slack lower lip as she pauses on the verge of speaking. Today she is brazen. She tells me people are having a drink, asks would I like to come.

I look up at her, I put my pencil down. It's perverse, the way I enjoy making her uncomfortable. I lace my fingers together behind my head and lean back. She smiles a searching smile. "No thanks," I tell her. "I've got plans." She sighs and pulls the door closed behind her.

Back in the neighborhood, I stop at the bar a few blocks from home. It's at the border between the downscale end and the blocks that are filling with prosperity. It's been there a long time, watching the money come and go. Behind the mahogany bar are glittering bottles and a mirror the size of the wall, framed in the same mahogany. I sit in the back. I don't want to be faced with my own image.

It's around nine by the time I gather my strength to go home. When I get to my stoop a man in a cheap suit gets out of a grey sedan, another shuts off the car and follows. I hurry into the vestibule. The first one knocks on the door's long glass panel. I press 9-1-1 on my phone and keep my finger over the call button. The landlord's dog is barking, deep and fast. I hope they can hear her. I open the door a little.

What happens is not what I'm expecting at all. He flashes a badge.

It takes me a while to equalize. I feel like I've stood up too fast. He must be used to that, the long moment of adjustment to the surprise of his presence on a doorstep. "Hi," I say finally. "Can I help you?"

It's strange how we revert to the language of service in the face of institutional authority. Can I help you. I have nothing to sell him. I don't want to help him. I distrust men with badges. But my deepest reflex is still one of deference as the leather cover of his badge flips closed. He doesn't ask my name.

"Do you know what trespassing is, little lady?"

"Yes."

"I got a report you've been messing around on somebody's property down by the canal." He holds up the lock and chain broken by Jimmy's bolt cutters. "Look familiar?"

"Are you charging me with something?"

"No sweetie pie, I'm *warning* you about something. We got a mutual friend, and he wants you out of his hair. You get the picture? You been told nicely to stay out of what all isn't your business. Isn't that right."

Dealer. This man, this cop, he's dealer's errand boy. "Yes," I say, and force myself to look him in the eye. What I am being shown here is that I have no recourse. I am on my own.

The cop reaches out and smoothes an errant lock of my hair behind my ear, a mother's gesture from which I flinch. "Then we understand each other. Be good, and you'll never see me again. Don't think about the alternative." He descends the front steps and gets back into his car.

I watch him drive away. Dealer with the cops in his pocket. Cinco and the empty lot. The house full of shadows. I go upstairs and perch in the frame of the back window, looking out toward the little street, trying to make the mismatched pieces fit.

7.

AT CERTAIN HOURS, like this one, midtown is just like the shift change in a factory town. A crowd spills out, merges briefly, overtakes the sidewalks and quickly disperses toward home. These are the nights when I catch sight of my brother stepping behind someone waiting at a far crosswalk, or pushing his way into the revolving door of a skyscraper. I've stopped following the mirage, and I've stopped running from it. But it's still his broken face I see when I feel the thread-thin tug of someone trailing behind me through a sea of strangers.

Now, back in the neighborhood, I can't shake the ghost. There's an hour of daylight still in the sky. I pick up a camera, and then I pull the old photograph out of the drawer where I keep it. The man in the picture never changes. He grins at me, his eyes shine. I slip the picture into my pocket.

Julio calls out to me from his corner. "Hi mami, taking the pictures again?"

"It's a compulsion," I say, and he nods, I'm not sure if his English stretches that far. "Julio, how long you been living here?"

"Since they kick me out of Spanish Harlem, mami. Long time."

"Did you know a guy named Cinco, in the old days here?"

He chuckles. "Five-o? No lady, I know nobody Cinco here."

I take a deep breath and slide the picture out of my pocket. The risk is only more suspicion, and I've crossed that line already with startling finality. "Do you know this guy?"

Julio crosses his arms high over his drooping gut. "Did you get a new job, mami?"

I jerk a thumb over my shoulder. "No," I say. I'm ready for this one. "I found it in the house. There was a box of stuff in the closet."

He runs his tongue under his upper lip, the moustache quivers. "He's nobody to me."

I nod, keep walking. I pass by the little street, it's deserted. I go on down to the first bridge over the canal and stop in the middle to take a few pictures of the oily and shimmering water. I loop back around by the projects. The man with the sling is rocking back and forth on his feet, looking around. His eyes look pretty lucid. "Hi lady," he says. "How you doin' today?"

"I'm fine, thanks. Out for a walk." I take the picture out of my pocket and show it to him. "This guy look familiar to you?"

He tips his head one way, then another. "That's a pretty old picture."

"Yeah."

"You lookin' for somebody?"

"I found a box of old stuff in the basement of my building. I'm just curious. I guess he used to live there." It's at least plausible, and most of the neighborhood already thinks I'm strange.

He just shrugs.

"Maybe someone else would know?"

He looks off into the distance a while. "I don't know. He's white, you know? Nobody I know keeps much track of y'all. Except you, with that hair. Everybody sees you."

My face goes hot, I know a flush is spreading over it. "Yeah, thanks," I manage to say and turn away.

I must have expected fortuity, but I need a better angle. So I walk toward the river and knock at Vasquez's door.

He opens the ironwork gate that guards his entryway. "You again." He squints, his head jutting forward as if pulled by his nose. "Red, that's good. You look better without the wig."

"Thanks." I smile. I'm no more than a foot away from him, and once again it feels like he might reach out his good arm and rest his hand on my ass, begin to ease me into a slow swaying dance.

He leans back against the door frame. "You want the apartment after all? Or maybe you just couldn't stop thinking about me, huh?"

"I was hoping you could help me with something."

"Depends what it is."

"I just want to ask you something."

"I'll answer any question you ask, Red."

I hand him the picture. "Do you know who this is?"

He holds it up. "That's Madder. Guy who bought my building. He who you're looking for? If I knew that, I woulda told you to quit before."

A tremor of emptiness moves through me. "You mean because he's dead. That's what you told me before."

"Dead, gone, what's the difference."

"Which one?" My voice breaks.

He reaches out and touches my shoulder. "Okay, gone, last I heard. What do you want with him? He's an old man now."

"I have something that belongs to him."

"How do you know it's his if you don't even know the guy?"

I don't answer him. I can see he doesn't believe me and I don't know what else to say.

He looks over my shoulder, waves at a neighbor. "Whatever it is I'm sure he doesn't need it. Throw it away." There's something new in his tone, clipped and cold. "Anyway, you shouldn't be asking around about a guy like Madder."

"Why not. What's he done?"

"He's the usual suspect, a hand in everybody else's pie, women lying for him all over town. I'm telling you. That building I had, it burned when Madder owned it. Not once, twice. The man's got no ethics at all. Loose cannon. Men do what they do, but not in their own neighborhood."

"Are you saying he burned it down?"

"I'm not saying anything except he's no prince."

I nod. This is supposed to deter me, but Vasquez's elusiveness only pulls me in deeper. Here's a new blank space in the story that cries out to be filled. "Do you know where he is now?"

"Far away, if he's got any brains. Too many backs he stabbed down here."

"I have to find him."

"I don't get you. You don't know the guy and I told you he's a mother-fucker but you got this major need to find him?"

"I can't explain."

"Try me."

Now the silence is mine. Compulsion doesn't fit into words, neither does the ache it soothes. "It feels wrong to keep it and wrong to just throw it away." I tell him finally. "So I'm stuck."

"That's the stupidest reason I ever heard."

From upstairs, his sister's voice, calling him to dinner like she'd call a little boy. He shrugs and locks the door behind him. "You know how hard it is to find someone who don't want to be found?"

I nod. I want to tell him everything. I want to tell him I know it both ways, but I can't tell him a thing.

It's dark by the time I walk back through the projects. Dealer's on his corner, and I go by as fast as I can. He's got one of his boys backed up against the wall, one hand on the boy's shoulder and one his chest. "Don't tell me stories, son," he says. He's talking softly but with force, his tone all the more menacing for how controlled it is. "Don't tell me a story unless you was there. Do not," he says and pushes harder on the boy's chest, "Do *not* tell me the story of the story. You hear?"

—

Now the man in the picture has a name. Madder. The second-to-last man who owned the place the letter was sent to, who owned it when it burned. And this Madder, he was bad news in some unspecified way. A man who seemed not to work for his money. A man who had women in the palm of his hand, in the pocket of his coat. Where he has me now.

Walking home, there's an old man shuffling slowly along in front of me, his wrist leashed to an equally slow dog. He's going slow because he's old, certainly. But also he's reading a magazine, clutching it with two hands, the way a small child would hold a book. He's not very tall, I can see over his shoulder. It's porn.

The dog pulls at the leash, and the old man stops while it pisses on a scraggly sapling. They move on and he folds the magazine, tossing it into the public trash at the corner.

I stop at the corner bodega for a Coke. A small pregnant woman with a big voice comes in and says to no one in particular, "Where's my husband at?" She looks at the proprietor. "How come you don't know where my husband's at?"

"He's off today," the man says softly.

The woman turns to a tall black girl in gold heels and tight jeans. "You grown up," she says, louder than necessary in the cluttered aisle. "I saw you. You grown up to be a good lookin' girl."

The girl speaks softly too, the woman has stolen all the volume the room gets. "Thank you very much." She looks a little embarrassed.

"Where's my husband," the woman turns back to the proprietor. "You a bad father-in-law, how come you don't know where my husband is," she asks, cocking her hand on her hip. "Hmph." She doesn't leave him much room to answer. The man looks startled and shakes his head. She gives him a hard look and then, thinking better of the whole thing, she just sways her hips out the door.

I follow her out, and reach into my pocket to check that the picture's still there. Madder. I call information and ask for Edward Madder. Of course there's no listing for him. Nobody hides in plain sight. But there is one for Delores Madder. The address is in a neighborhood that used to be rough and no longer is, on the far side of a vast and gracious graveyard.

8.

I WAIT UNTIL SATURDAY. I can't turn up on an old woman's doorstep in the darkness after work. I get off the subway a stop early so I can get the feel of the neighborhood before I call on her. The streets are quiet here, with tall old apartment buildings along the boulevards and freestanding houses on the sidestreets. Delores Madder's house is brown, with a generous white porch wrapping around its side. There's a window open on the second floor, lights on in the back of the first floor. I ring the doorbell. No one answers. I knock, but the house is silent. Not even the creaking footsteps of someone ignoring the door. I walk around the side of the porch and peer through the old warped glass. It's a living room, there's a pile of knitting on the sofa and a full ashtray on the coffee table. Signs of life. I can see the entryway too, the inside face of the door. There's an odd thing there, mounted on the side molding. It's a little security camera.

Maybe she lives alone.

With the lights on and the window open, it seems likely she'll be back. I get a coffee on the boulevard and find a bench outside the graveyard. The light is filtering down through the diminishing leaves. People have their heads down, watching the sidewalk as they move along beaten paths to the day ahead. Across the street I see a woman, I think she is someone I haven't seen in fifteen years. Then she comes a little closer. It's not her at all. It was just the way she kept tucking her hair behind her ear.

After a while I start to catch a chill, so I walk a loop around her neighborhood, down along a wide, divided boulevard with grand apartment houses set back from the road. They've got names carved into the lintels of their entryways: the Mildred, the Diplomat, the Luxor. Architectural delusions of grandeur. The center median of the boulevard is lined with benches. Along each block there are a dozen people sitting and standing. They're crooked and old, bundled up, arguing, feeding pigeons, taking what sun there is to be taken. Maybe Delores is here, maybe she's one of those ladies in headscarves. A woman gets up and crosses the street toward me. She walks purposefully down the nearest cross street and then veers around a corner. She's walking up the street where Delores's house is, five or six blocks on. I follow her. She's slow and I get too close. So I stoop over, miming the actions of tapping a stone from my shoe. When I stand up, she's gotten to the corner of the big street just before Delores's block. She turns left, the wrong way.

"Shit," I say out loud. I wanted the woman to be her. I'm scouring the world for hidden messages. The woman who is not Delores hears me swearing and turns around. She spits into the gutter and keeps on.

I'm so close now, and impatient. It's been an hour and a half, I think. I cross over and walk up the steps. If she isn't there I'll have to come again another day. The street seems empty, but there's the camera, and there are always more eyes watching a quiet street than anyone imagines.

From the door I can see her, down the hall past the front stairwell, she's crossing the kitchen at the back of the house. She's small and thin, her shoulders rounded forward, succumbing inexorably to gravity. When I ring the bell she comes back into view and takes off the glasses she's got on a chain around her neck, squinting at me through the dim hallway. She wipes her hands on her apron, removes it, and walks toward me.

I smile at her, and I can feel how bright and false it looks. I'm not even sure what to say. She turns a deadbolt and opens the door. "Yes?"

I fumble in my pocket for the photograph and hold it out to her. "He's your son," I say, hoping it's true.

Her jaw sets and she takes a deep breath. "I have no son. I have a daughter."

But I can see the resemblance, now that I'm watching her face. She's got the same deep blue eyes, the same fine long nose.

"He looks just like you," I say.

Her lips pull tight, a hint of disgust. "He was my son once."

"What do you mean?"

"He's not welcome here."

I'm not either, her stiff, tall posture makes that clear. She's made herself impassable, and it's clear she's had some practice at it. I hold my ground. I don't say anything hoping she'll fill the silence.

"Who are you? You're not the usual type comes looking for him. He owes a nice clean girl like you money too?"

"No. I need to find him though."

"Look, I don't know what you're up to, but he's a deadbeat and I don't know where he is. And when I saw him last Jimmy Carter was the president."

She shuts the door and stands with her hands on her hips, waiting for me to leave. I stay where I am, holding her gaze through the warped glass. Tears are coming into my eyes, and they're real. I dig my thumbnail into my palm to still them. Weakness won't help here is what I'm thinking.

But I'm wrong. She opens the door again. "Well you can't just stand on my porch all day."

She's softening. I can see it written into the lines of her face. Loneliness, empathy she's tried hard to put down. I look down at my feet and then into her eyes again. I am harmless. "Please? Tell me a little about him."

She lets me in and waves me into the front parlor. She comes back with a bottle of gin and two glasses of ice. It tastes like metal.

"He's too old to have broken your heart, I hope to God."

"It's not that. I have something that's his. I want to give it back."

"Where'd you get this thing of his?"

She's not asking what it is. She doesn't want to know. Like everything else she's said, it doesn't speak well of him. "Someone left it for me. It's complicated."

"How'd you get mixed up with him in the first place?"

"I'm not. I mean, I've never met him."

She draws her chin back into her neck, squints an eye at me. All skepticism looks this way. I'm not getting anywhere. "You want some truth from me," she says. "Truth takes an even trade."

What happens instead is I tell her something that feels like the truth, but it's a lie as big as any I've ever told. "It's my brother. He's gone."

"What'd he run from? Gambler?"

"No, drugs. An addict. I gave up on him and now he's gone and I can't live with it anymore."

She lays a warm hand on my shoulder. "They'll take everything you've got, honey. You did right. You leave it lie now. You can't help him."

"I know that. But I can't live with it either." It's true except that I know exactly where to find him. I know which corner and I know which woman's run-down apartment and I know the plasma bank and I know the kind mechanic who gives him work every time he tries to get clean. What's true is my sorrow, my crumbling resolve.

"What's Edward got to do with it?"

"I found the picture in my brother's room, with a letter. It said something about a piece of out of town work."

"But the picture's so old."

"Yes," I fill in the blanks as fast as they appear. "The letter said so. It said, 'add an extra lifetime, but you'll recognize the eyes.' I can imagine that's true." I look into hers, the same stunning blue.

"I wish I could help you. But the last time I saw him was his sister's funeral. I washed my hands of him after that."

"What happened to her?"

Her lips set hard. She lets the question settle and drift away. "For years there were men coming around looking for him. They threatened me but I'm not afraid of them. Nobody brings violence to this block. It's watched over."

I can tell she doesn't mean the police. "The camera."

"It doesn't work. We've all got them here though. Fakes, every one."

"Symbols work."

"When there's something to back them up they do."

"Who came looking?"

"People he owed. People he crossed. Women he left."

Her pure contempt echoes between us. All I can think is what a charmer he must be. "So you don't know where he is?'

"I make it my business not to."

"Is this where he grew up?"

"No. I moved here after my daughter died. This was my uncle's house. He died too. Everybody dies. I'm here alone now."

The daughter. Each resolution carries another mystery inside it. Delores screws the top back on the bottle of gin.

"You did the right thing when you cut your brother off. I know you won't listen to me, but forgetting him is the best thing you can do for yourself."

"Did it work for you?"

"I'm tired," she says, "You get to be my age and just the sound of the stars setting wakes you."

She shows me to the door. The house creaks as if it were just as tired as she.

———

When I get home, Natalie is waiting on the stoop in a stream of afternoon sun. "You're late," she says. "I was about to leave."

I pat my pocket and discover I left my phone at home. Natalie too is lonely, and acutely aware of flagging attention. I lean into her disappointment. "I'm sorry," I tell her.

She's got a camera around her shoulder. "Let's walk, the light is good." She heads across the projects and I follow her down the long residential street on the other side, waiting for her to walk off the little prideful injury. One of the bodegas over here is gone. I'm standing in front of the drawn metal shutters trying to remember when I last saw it open. A few days, a week, maybe. A big man with a little dog trailing passes by shaking his head. "Ain't right," he says. "Hurt's comin' down."

Natalie is halfway down the block, talking to an old woman who has parked herself in a lawn chair in front of her building, swaddled in sweaters, taking in the last of the sun. I can see the negotiation from here, the woman shaking her head and playfully waving Natalie away, Natalie's innocent shrug, the woman's surrender. Natalie kneels down and lifts her camera. What will come of it is not unlike the aerial landscapes she shoots, but now it's the face, abstracted as a landscape seen from above, a pattern of lines and divots and hills. She backs up and takes another one at a more flattering distance, the one she'll send to the woman. She's just writing down the woman's address when I catch up.

"She wouldn't like the close-up," I say. "None of them would. What happens when you show them someday?"

"I'll never show these."

"Why not?"

She's quiet a moment, we walk a block or so that way. "It's a collection," she says finally. I can't argue with that.

Natalie turns down toward the canal, and I think of taking her to the little street, to the empty lot, and telling her the story. It's unfolded before her averted eyes, the photograph, the databases, the bureaucratic phone calls. She has asked and I haven't explained. I could now.

"How many portraits do you take in a week?"

"One a day. You know that."

Maybe she's right, maybe I already knew, but the ritual looks different to me now. What I see is how like animals we are, every one of us. We do things, we are compelled to, we can't stop, we don't know why.

When the light is too low to clear the buildings, Natalie packs up her camera and I walk her to the subway. Heading home, I'm walking fast and feeling sour about the inexorable shortening of the day. There are two big women on a bench, a third standing before them leaning into her speech like a preacher. "We're Christians," she says. "We're not supposed to wear jeans."

As I rush around my corner, I almost plow over three men with parkas over their pajamas, each pulled along the sidewalk by a dachshund on a leash.

Now I'm free. I run up the stairs and call Vasquez. He told me he'd answer any question I asked, and I've come to a new one. The phone rings a long time. I imagine him staring at the unfamiliar number on the phone's display, deciding. Finally he picks up.

"It's me," I say.

"You just can't get enough, can you, Red?"

"I talked to his mother."

"You're a selfish girl, you know that? Bothering people in their homes." It's a slap, and it's one I've had coming. "I'm sorry."

It's a long time before he says anything. I'm not even sure he's still there until I hear an ambulance screaming in the background. "You can play your game with me, but why don't you leave the old ladies out of it from now on." Unwittingly he has become my partner, he knows he is culpable now.

My head sinks into my waiting palm. There is no real medicine for shame.

His voice comes softer now. "You called me for something besides a talking to, what was it?"

"There's something I didn't tell you last time," I say. The lie comes easier with repetition. I almost believe it now. "I'm looking for my brother. I found the picture in his things."

"What happened to him?"

"He got mixed up in some trouble. I've run out of options. Madder is my last hope."

"That's a hard place to be."

"That's why I called. You said you had an army buddy. The one who introduced you to Madder. Maybe he knows where to find him."

"Another door for you to knock on."

"The last one, I promise."

He's quiet again, all I can hear is the squeak of sneakers on a wooden floor. He's pacing, and I know he's giving in. "You want Joe Bonner. He works down by the docks, over on the Polishtown side of the river. I haven't seen him for a couple of years, but if I wanted to find him I'd try at the bar next to the Coast Guard station, around closing time."

"He's the last one."

"You're gonna have to wait a few weeks. He takes his vacation this time of year. Hunts deer upstate."

"Thank you," I say. I should be more grateful, but I feel as though I've earned it.

"Don't say I sent you."

"Why not?"

"It's not exactly ethical, what I'm doing with you here."

I wait a beat. "What's he look like?"

"He's a big guy, eyes like a basset hound. Walks with a limp." He pauses. "Nobody got out of there whole."

"Is he white or black?"

"Black. You know what? I might not have told you if you hadn't asked. You should quit while you're ahead, you know that, right?"

"I know," I say, and the truth of it feels heavy as iron. If I could stop, I would. And that's what I tell him.

It's only late afternoon, but it feels like weeks since yesterday.

And so I wait for the moment to come. There are dull things to occupy my hands and still my racing mind. I wash the dishes, I carry the laundry to the corner and leave it for the squat Columbian woman to wash. Back home, there's a stack of sweaters the moths have ravaged, I've been planning to mend them for weeks. I weave the needle in and out of the threads I've laid. The holes vanish.

NOVEMBER

9.

IN THE WAITING DAYS I am blind to the life of the streets. It seems that all I ever sought there was Madder, that all my days I have been looking for him, in every city, on every block I walked.

Now Jimmy lies beside me, and turns up onto his elbow, giving me all his scrutiny. He draws a hand down my face, closing my eyes the way you might close a dead person's eyes. "You don't see me, do you?"

I don't open my eyes. "What do you mean?"

"I mean that you're going away somewhere, and you're taking pieces of me with you." He's touching my hair softly, and I feel a warm tear wash over my cheek. His.

"I'm here," I say. It's not just him, but he can't know that. It's every speck of the known world I've let go of. I feel how my inward turn cuts him. The cuts bleed, and something I never expected happens. His rawness draws me closer, against all necessity, against my will. I fit the heel of my hand into the hollow between his ribs. "I'm right here," I say, pushing against his heart.

10.

I HAVE THE DAY MARKED on my calendar. The legal limit of deer hunting season. A week before the moment comes I lose all hunger, and too the desire to sleep. Penance, purification, my bodily instincts take on meaning. Jimmy's worried fingers graze the circles under my eyes. He thinks he sees pain, but I feel as peaceful as a monk.

When the day comes I ride the commuter rail, watching the city's sprawl fly by. At the last stop, I get off and walk toward the smell of the sea. The bar is there as Vasquez said it would be, hard by the water, at the edge of the world. Inside, it's all stale air and dark wood. Four men hunch over the counter, nodding at the television, sighing into their drinks. There's a phone booth in the back, wooden, with a collapsing door. Inside is a girl sitting on the little seat, her biker boot propped up against the crook of the door. At a back table, there's a skinny guy in a hoodie, reading Proust. Things are smashing against each other here, the neighborhood churning over. It's the apex of the transition, when the working men and the idle youth misspend their hours side-by-side. I pay for a shot and sit at the bar with the old men. I've come here with questions, I can't play it off as a coincidence. All I can do is wait for the man with the hangdog eyes to show up, and ask.

The old man next to me touches my wrist and speaks without turning toward me. "Let me tell you something. Don't ever get any older than you are right now. It's rotten. The body betrays you," he says and bangs a cane I hadn't noticed hard against the bar.

"I'll try," I tell him.

He waves at the fat bartender. "Get her another one, whatever she's got."

The bartender pours another shot into my glass and raps his knuckles on the bar, signaling that the drink isn't mine to pay for. I clink glasses with the old man and thank him. He hands me the newspaper that's folded in front of him. "I don't know what you came here for but I know you're not here to chit chat with these old bones."

I take the paper. "Cheers," I say and resettle myself in an empty booth. I stare at the paper but there's too much anticipation running through me, and I wind up rereading the same sentence over and over, turning a page, fixing on a different line, still without comprehension. All the while I'm imagining what will happen when Bonner turns up. If he does.

The boy reading Proust packs up and wanders away. The girl emerges from the phone booth, I'd forgotten her. She's been in there half an hour, maybe more. The side of her face is red from the pressure of her cell phone against her ear. She slams the folding door shut and stomps back into the room. Two of the old men go outside, smoke a while, and come back, bringing wisps of the rancid smoke in with them.

The bartender holds a remote up in the air toward the TV, scanning through channels until he lights on a football game. I'm on my third whiskey when Bonner walks in. It's the eyes, of course, the eyes betrayed by gravity. That's how I know him. He pulls a stool up to the bar, the bartender pulls him a beer from the tap. He lays down a twenty and leaves the change in front of him on the bar, he'll be here a while. I stand up and approach the bar. I lean in next to him and ask for another shot. I'm already a little tipsy, and it's a good thing.

"Excuse me," I say, in the upward lilt of a question.

He doesn't look up from his beer. "We know each other from somewhere?"

"No, but I wanted to talk to you."

He turns now and faces me. The round eyes sag, and the crevices curving down from the sides of his nose to his mouth are deep and dark. He takes off his tweed cap and rests it on the bar, settling in. "About what?"

There isn't any way to make this casual, so I press right to the point. "I'm looking for Madder."

"Don't know anybody by that name," he says, draining his beer and plunking his glass in the bar's gutter to show the bartender he wants another.

"From the army. You were in the army together."

"Not me."

"Are you sure," I ask, stupidly. I was prepared for refusal, but not this.

He reaches over the bar and picks up a pen, a napkin. He writes an address. He writes a time, it's a few hours from now.

"Try this guy. He comes here too. The other black guy. Somebody gave you a bad tip."

I stuff the napkin in my pocket. "Okay, thanks. Sorry to bother you."

"No bother," he says and turns his attention back to the beer before him.

I put on my coat and walk out the door.

—

Two hours later I come to the stoop of the address on the napkin and knock. It's Bonner at the door. "All right, come on in. You don't ask a man things like that in a public venue."

"I'm sorry, I didn't think it was anything much, just looking for your old friend."

"That's a man's own business."

"Thanks for helping me"

"I haven't yet."

"You know him."

"Army, like you say."

"Do you know where he is now?"

"You know lady, you're not the first person come looking for Madder. Lotta people want a piece of him."

"What do you mean?"

"You meet him, he's the life of the party. All charming, full of schemes that sound like everybody's ticket out. Then it's watch your wife, watch your wallet, watch your bank account. Leaves people with empty hands when they're supposed to be full."

"So he cheats people and they come looking for you?"

"We were partners."

"Partners at what?"

"Things."

"Why did you quit?"

"Got tired of cleaning up his messes."

"So what happens when people come looking?"

"I tell them 'you find him I want a piece.'"

"Why?"

"He owes me."

"So you protect him?"

"He owes me money. The day he's got some I wanna be first in line for it."

"Who comes after him?"

"Who doesn't."

"Are you afraid of them?"

"Lady, I'm afraid of nobody. But I don't take chances, either." He sighs, and his eyes do too. "What do you want with him, anyway? He owe you too?"

"No. I found something that's his."

His glance rakes me over, up and down. "How do you know he wants it back?"

"He might not. I don't know." I want this man's respect, somehow. I won't get it. The only story I have for him is a story of weakness, desperation. I spin it out for him. Like Vasquez, like Delores, the lie that feels true begins to soften him.

"Shit," he says. "He's not even that hard to find. Men come looking for him are punks. He's in a Section 8 house way uptown. Terrific Tenements. Cruel joke, right?"

What startles me is how little satisfaction I take from what I've just learned. He's not in front of me yet. But he's close now, this man made of flesh and false promises. A jolt of nausea runs through me.

Bonner holds his metal screen door open for me and sends me out into a sudden, shivering rain. It lasts the whole long train ride, and drenches me as I hurry from the station to my house. At home I step into a hot shower to shake the chill, but it won't abate. At last I give up. I dry off and listen to the water churning down the drain, then I crawl under the covers. The chase was an abstraction until it materialized into coordinates. I lay sleepless through the long night, imagining myself at last in a room with Madder, aging him in my mind like a police sketch. When dawn comes I drift off into a sharp, vivid morning dream. I wake to find it's all taken place in the space of an hour, the city is still creaking to life. In the dream I have, none of this has happened. In the dream I have, I take the letter back to the post office. In the dream I have, I never even find the vacant lot.

—

No dabs of powder can conceal my weariness at the office as the day churns by. My eyes are Bonner's eyes, puffy, shadowed, hollow. I cross paths with my assistant in the bathroom, and for once she draws a tight breath and speaks directly. "You look like a truck ran over you last night. Are you okay?"

I look up, and draw my face into a placid calm. "I'm fine." I offer no explanation, no mitigation.

"Oh," she says. Now she's awkward. I haven't responded with a confession. "I thought, nevermind." She disappears into a stall and I hear the slippery sound of her skirt lining against her skin as she slides it up. When I get back to my desk, I see an improbable thing. It's hardly winter yet and it has started to snow. I lean over the contract I'm proofing and focus on each word individually. I find no mistakes, which isn't possible. I start over. This time the mistakes shimmer.

When it's time to go home, the snow has just stopped falling and everything glitters in the darkness. Out on the sidewalk, behind me someone is singing, she sings a little off key but everyone knows the song anyway: "a beautiful sight... we're happy tooonight... walkin' in a winter wonderland." A few passersby from the other direction smile. I turn around. There's a woman in a parka, she's maybe fifty, or she has smoked all her life and is younger than that. She's got her arm hooked into the elbow of a man in a hoodie, she's leaning in tight, smiling like a child caught sneaking something small but illicit. She catches my eye.

"It's a good song," I say as they pass me by. She laughs and laughs and I stay still and listen to her until they round the corner and drift away.

I stop at the butcher's back in the neighborhood. I want some of the good pasta he sells. He's young, the butcher, already bald, with eyes that are a little sad. It must have been his father's shop once, or his uncle's. His hands have an intimacy with the countertops, he has been back there his whole life. He works with knives, he works with death, although he doesn't think of it that way. And the thing is he's got the sweetest voice, low and gentle and full of something that sounds like love, but can't possibly be. When you need someone to tell you that everything is going to be okay, it's his voice you want, shhh honey it's all gonna work out fine.

I wish I believed him. I swing out through the door back onto the street. I hear a man's voice sing out, "You cookin' me dinner, baby?" It's Dealer.

"I thought you were cooking for me."

"I don't cook for any woman."

He's losing his smile. He takes me by the arm like a gentleman, but there's force behind it. "I'm gonna walk you home," he says.

I'm tired of playing along. "What do you want?"

"You're wearing out your welcome, know what I mean?"

"I'm not bothering you."

"You stirring a lot of things up these days. Time to stop."

"You keep telling me that. Got something to hide?"

"Don't push me, woman. I'm a man of business and you best stay out of it."

"What makes you think I'm interested in your business?"

"You askin' too many questions outta too many people around here."

"If I was a narc, would I be that clumsy?"

"I don't know what you are, but you pissing me off, and you gonna stop, or you gonna move."

I shake my arm free from his grip. I don't know what he thinks I'm doing, but it doesn't matter now. I'm almost done. I have no questions left for the neighborhood. I have one last errand. Then it's over.

11.

IT TAKES ME all week to work up to the trip. I make excuses to myself each night as I'm leaving the office. I'm tired, the laundry is waiting. I promised the night to Jimmy. Tomorrow, I say. Tomorrow.

When Saturday comes, I run out of reasons not to go. I sleep until my bones ache and then I ride the subway to the northernmost tip of the city. The train's running local and it takes almost two hours. The air in the subway is close, it's got everyone sniffing idly. At the end of the car, there are two brown-haired girls in identical dresses, a couple of sizes apart. The older one's hair is straight and her face plain, with a downward turn at the corner of her brown eyes. The younger one has a halo of curls, a face like a heart, and eyes the color of wet slate. She spins around the pole while her sister watches mournfully from her proper seat. It will always be like this between them.

It is a day of doubling. When I change to the local halfway through the journey, I sit across from two boys, brothers, with hazel eyes, creamed coffee skin and halos of long kinky hair that's just a shade darker. The older one plays guitar by the doors, the younger one sits on the bench and plays bongos, it's a halfhearted rendition of "Norwegian Wood." The drummer's fingers are gifted, and he is languid. He takes off his glasses with one hand, tucking them into his shirt, still tapping out the beat with the other. The song ends far short of the coming stop. The tips are collected in a plastic bag. The train jerks across the bridge. The boy puts his drums aside and makes a fist, which he tries ambitiously to shove into his mouth.

He knows I've been watching him. I ask, "Does it fit?" He shakes his head. He tries again, first compressing the fist with his other hand and stretching his mouth to its limit. "Ouch," he says softly to no one, pulling his hand away. "That hurt." There is one final attempt, again falling short of success. The train slows into the station, and he slides out after his brother just as the doors are closing.

It's been more than an hour by the time I ride the long narrow escalator up to the street. I step aside from the subway entrance to get my bearings. The massive intersection is disjointed, as though opposing teams of planners laid their boulevards in spite of each other. I imagine the battle of backhoes and steamrollers, the dump trucks and the battalions of scrappy men facing off like rival gangs. The strangely angled corners are full of discount stores and Caribbean diners. I duck into one of the diners and get a paper cup of cafe con leche, sweet and hot. I get some skeptical looks too. I ask the voluptuous young woman who makes the coffee if she can point me to the street I'm looking for. She shrugs one shoulder. I wait. She points to a man at the end of the counter and calls out to him in Creole. He's old and bowed, methodically eating a plate of chicken and yellow rice. He straightens up a little and looks me over. He points out the glass front of the restaurant at the adjacent street and counts as his finger moves around the intersection, "One, two, three, four," and then his hand springs open, the gesture a magician makes just before he reaches into the hat and removes the rabbit. Poof.

I walk slowly around the four crossings, pacing myself to match the leisurely strolling of the neighborhood's women, their asses swaying and their hands on their hips. This one has curlers bound by a kerchief, that one is pushing a cart full of groceries. I slow even more as I turn the corner and approach my destination, the end of the line, the end of the story. No matter how slowly you pace yourself, eventually you arrive.

The building is brick, utilitarian. Six stories, about as high as you can ask a person to climb. On the third floor there are men perched sideways on the sill of each window, taking in the air. The rooms must be only a single window wide. Space for a narrow bed, a chest of drawers. Maybe there's a mirror, a hotplate, a few chipped dishes. I go in.

The security desk is fronted with yellowed plexiglass, bulletproof certainly, but also knife-proof and fist-proof and riot-proof. Nothing is anger-proof, and now there's a man pounding on the plexi shouting in Spanish. I hear the words for "motherfucker" and "money," but I can't parse the rest of it. I stay in the doorway, under the protection of the lintel. I could still leave easily. After a minute a fat man shuffles over and thwacks the angry one on the meat of his shoulder. Angry guy's hands stop, and then his voice stops too. The fat man points at me and waves the angry man away.

"You need something, honey? You here to see somebody I guess."

"Yeah," I say, still cautious, still in the doorway. "I'm here to see Madder."

"Sixth floor," he says, and knocks on the plexi. "Sign in."

I write my name in a ledger and the security guard buzzes me through the double doors down the hallway. "Six D. Halfway down."

I wonder if they'll get the word up to him before I can scale the stairs. I'm speeding up now that I'm almost there, sprinting. By the time I get to the top I'm a little out of breath. I stay in the dank stairwell, waiting for the rhythms of my body to settle. I stop gasping, but my heart won't slow down. It's not going to. I go to the door. I knock.

A lock tumbles, the door opens a crack and there's a weathered face bisected by a brass chain. "What do you want?"

I've imagined this moment over and over. I know what to do, but not what happens next. I hold up the photograph for him to see. The door closes, there's the sound of the chain sliding out. The door opens and the man steps back. His hair is still wild as when the wind lifted it in the photograph, but it's flocked with gray now. His eyes are still bluer than the sky.

He's wearing just a saggy undershirt, the small room has gathered too much heat from the knocking radiator. "Sit down," he says and points to the old wooden desk chair across from the bed. Somewhere in his body, bones crackle as he takes a seat at the edge of the bed, facing me.

I hand him the photograph. He takes it indifferently, he's not accustomed to commenting on such things. It takes him a moment. He looks back at me.

"Handsome, eh?" He's shaking his head, smiling with just the corner of his mouth. The visage of a man caught by a memory.

"Who took the picture?"

"What do you want with it?"

"Turn it over."

He flips the picture with a quick twist of his wrist. He nods. "Where did you find this?"

I take the envelope out of my bag and hand it to him. "It found me."

"Come again?"

I point to the address. "That's around the corner from my house. It ended up in my mailbox a few months ago."

"It's 25 years old."

"I know."

"Ghost mail." He lays both on the bed next to him and turns his sharp blue eyes on me. "Okay, so. What?"

"Who took the picture?"

"I missed the part where you got a right to know my shit. You're overdoing the Good Samaritan routine, but hey, thanks." He raps a knuckle on the picture.

"You don't know what it took to find you."

"Oh, I can imagine. I make it my business not to be found. What's it to you?"

He thinks I'm a fool, wasting my time looking for a washed up grifter. And I am, I see that more plainly now, sitting in the squalid room across from a crumpled man. "What's the harm," I ask him. "What's the harm if you tell me the story." I can't explain to him how the bountiful error of the postal service felt like fate to me. "The picture found me, and I found you."

I pull my hair around over one shoulder and cross my legs on the awkward chair. I look down. I try to imagine that the broken man in front of me is the captivating man in the photograph. I raise my eyes to meet his, and what I give him now is unfettered longing. I catch my breath as I watch his hands stroke the surface of the photograph.

Men are all the same, that's what I think as I see his body soften, as his shoulders shift to line up with mine. Men can all be played.

"Damn this is ancient history," he starts. "A woman named Penny took it." He's gazing off into the past. "She had hair like yours. Fake red. She wore black boots. I knew her from high school, from before. Before the hair, before the boots. She was a cheerleader, and then she ran off somewhere. She came back to the neighborhood when her mom got sick."

"So she was your girlfriend?"

"Yeah."

"Where were you?"

"Not sure. I remember her taking it, she was laying on the ground. I think it was a parking lot. It was somewhere you don't lay down."

None of this is telling me the story I came to hear. "Why does it say that on the back, what did you have?"

He looks out the window a while, back down at the picture. He turns it over again. There's something about the way he's letting his pensiveness settle in, prolonging it. I believe that he's thinking. I also suspect he's performing.

"It's Penny's handwriting." He leans forward, props his forearms on his thighs. He looks at the floor. "I didn't know."

"You didn't know what?"

"God damn her."

"What happened?"

He gives me a tough face again, a 'why would I tell you anything' face. But then he does. "I guess it doesn't matter now. There was this guy Cinco. He used to be a cop. Worked Vice, got caught taking kickbacks, but they smoothed it over. Department had a bad reputation that way. So they just retire him, and he sets up as a private detective. Crazy thing, getting a license, with black marks like that on your record, you know? Anyways, that's Cinco. So one night, I think this is 1980 maybe. Everybody's down at the bar, and Cinco starts bragging about how much he milked out of the dealers back in Vice. Naming sums. Then he's got himself in a bragging mood. He tells how the other day he got hired by a city councilman to catch his wife cheating. But Cinco thinks he's real smart, so he follows the politician too. Caught him with his own side dish."

"And so Cinco's high as a kite, he's been telling the story, we're buying him drinks, and I don't even know how he could still stand up. He's a genius, he says. He blackmails the politician, gets ten thousand bucks. That was a shitload back then. He's got it stashed in a locker at the train station. How he's gonna hit the road. Gotta be six people heard all this. Me and Penny both. But you know, we all heard it, so whatcha gonna do."

"But somebody did something."

"The thing was, Cinco didn't remember telling us. Penny was real smooth, she teased him a few days later about how he was shooting off at the mouth. She says you told us all about the dealers you swindled at Vice, which of course, that ain't what he told us at all. He doesn't remember a word of it. So she starts sugaring him up. She gets him drunk and fucks him, and searches his apartment, while he sleeps it off. She finds the key to the locker. She keeps looking. She needs the locker number. Sharp girl. There's a calendar on the wall, it's showing two months ahead, and there's a date circled. December ninth. She takes a guess. She goes to locker 129, and damn if she's right. She calls and tells me to wait a week and then meet her at the public library in this little town upstate."

"Did she run out on you?"

"I wish. She turned up floating in the canal three days later. The man was a private detective. Jesus." He fans the air with the photograph.

"So what does that mean," I say, pointing to it.

"It means she tried to pin it on me. I guess it got lost in the mail. She sure wasn't going to be waiting at the library like she said she was."

"Why not just tell him herself?"

"You don't rat on people around here."

"What happened to Cinco?"

"He tried to run but he didn't run fast enough. He's upstate for life."

"He would have killed you if he found you?"

"I don't know. I didn't have the key or the money, and I knew she did. That's something to bargain with. Maybe she thought she was buying herself some time leading him to me. Enough time to get away. Stupid cunt."

He stands up and walks over to the window. When he turns back around, he's got a smile that's glowing with rage. This is what it really means to look devilish, I think.

He reaches under the bed for a bottle and offers me a shot of whiskey. I take it. I don't know what to say. I don't know why he's smiling like that, but for a moment the hair on the back of my neck bristles. He tips his whiskey back and takes a beer from the small fridge. I tip mine back too. He doesn't offer me a chaser. He sits back down on the bed, the smile still ruling his face.

"You know, this was all so long ago," he says, disingenuous now, with mocking eyes. "I'm not sure I told it right." He stares at the picture, at his younger self. He closes his eyes.

I wait. The whiskey warms me, I feel my skin responding to the warmed blood, the little current of fear settles itself.

Madder stands up and starts pacing in the narrow room. I turn my knees to the side to clear him space. Now he talks without looking at me.

"It's like I said before. A woman named Penny took the picture. She was with this guy Carlos, but she had me on the side. Carlos was a bag man for the neighborhood bookie, name of Sammy. Carlos ran the bar we all went to. That's where I met Penny. Bottle blonde like all the girls in the neighborhood back then, but she had these green eyes, all bright and full of trouble. She was like Eve holding an apple, you know?"

"Carlos was who all the girls wanted, but I could talk them into bed anyway. And Carlos had a bar to tend. It didn't take me long to reel her in. He opened every day at four. I talked my way into her bed every afternoon for weeks and kept on drinking Carlos's beer every night. Who takes pictures of their infidelities? Stupid women do."

"This kind of thing can't go on forever. Too good to last. Penny got sloppy. She started flirting with me at the bar in front of Carlos this one night. He sent her home and I didn't like to think about what was gonna happen to her when he closed up that night. Nothing good. But I didn't think about it for long, because then Cinco comes in. Cinco was a Vice cop, usually nobody wants to hang around with a cop, but Cinco was from the neighborhood, and his specialty was drugs. So the Vice cop drinks in the bookie's bar, and nobody bats an eyelash. Carlos had to pay him off a little, and he resented it like hell. One night Cinco gets himself extremely drunk and starts bragging about the money he took off a dealer last week. How he and his partner split it up and turned the guy loose. Ten thousand dollars he tells us, and you know that was a lot of money in those days. We all heard him. He goes stumbling out, everybody's calling odds on whether the story is true or not. I hear Carlos say to somebody, "He's gotten more than that off me all these years.""

I'm struggling to understand what's happening, to keep the surprise off my face. What I know for sure is I'm being rooked. I try to look at him the way a mother looks at a lying child. I should get up and leave. But I want to know why he's doing it. I raise my eyebrows at his brief silence.

"Couple days later the news on the street is somebody broke into Cinco's place, money's gone. Cinco's out for blood. Meanwhile, Penny's on my doorstep in tears, she shows me the bruises on her arms. Carlos beat her up, she says, whipped her with his belt and made her confess about her and me, and she's afraid for both of us. She runs off to her sister's upstate, like he can't find her there. I go across the river and hide out at my army buddy's place a while. Nobody from the neighborhood knows him. I stay away four days. On the fourth day I call my uncle. He says Cinco accused Carlos of stealing the money. I guess somebody else heard him say that about all the protection money he paid. Next thing anybody knows Cinco turns up drowned in the canal. They say he was dead already. Knife wound. Everybody knew it had to be Carlos but nobody's gonna rat on him. Had it coming one way or another, that's what everybody thought."

"That's Carlos's handwriting on the back of the picture. On this too," he says, touching the envelope. "I saw him writing up our tabs every night for years."

"So now you're saying this guy Carlos tried to frame you. Penny had nothing to do with it."

He's grinning. "You sound like you don't believe me."

"I don't think you want me to believe you."

Again, the devil's smile. "Why did you come here?"

What confidence I have left unravels. I can't admit the answer, so I tell him something that is also true. "I told you, I wanted to know," I say. "Wouldn't you?"

"I want a story, I watch TV, lady."

"Everybody told me something different about you. A mystery. I guess I was playing detective."

He snorts and drinks the last slug of his beer, takes another from the fridge. "You're a load of crap."

All the sudden I realize how little I have to lose, how crystalline and unrepeatable this moment is. "Bonner told me you took money off everyone in town, ran out on debts. He said he never told anyone where you were because if you had any money he wanted to get to you first."

"That so."

"That's what he said."

"He would say that. It's him owes me now."

"What does he owe you."

Madder flips the picture in his fingers, and begins again. "Honestly I don't remember who took this. It was up on the wall at the bar with a hundred other pictures, all the regulars had a few up there. It started with this girl Penny. She looked like Rita Hayworth, that black hair, the body. She was the, whatcha call it, like the cocktail waitress only it wasn't that fancy a place. But she was with Carlos and he liked to keep his eye on her. So she brought drinks to the folks who sat at the tables, or when it was busy she backed him up behind the bar. Anyway, she started it with the pictures, she got a Polaroid thing for her birthday and one night she took a picture of everybody who came in. She turned the whole bar upside down looking for a roll of tape and started decorating the walls. Then everybody started bringing in pictures. It was like a really really sad family album. A bunch of no-accounts and drunks."

He's talking slower this time. It seems like he's seeing things replayed in his mind's eye, but maybe I just want it to be that way. To gain some purchase on the messy tapestry of stories he's weaving around me. He's quiet for a while, so I prompt him. "Was Bonner there?"

"Bonner? No. Bonner was a gambler. Horses, football, whatever was up on the board. Bookie Sam was Carlos's boss, but Bonner didn't do business in the bar. Sammy had guys all over the city collecting for him. And Bonner owed him. He was in deep."

"Carlos collected on Fridays. He'd go around shaking guys down and then come back and open the bar. Throw the cash in the register and take it to Sammy's office in the morning, every week, the same procedure."

"Bonner's scared out of his mind, he says they're coming to break his fingers and shit. He wants me to talk to Carlos. No percentage in that, I tell him. Then I think of something useful. What I think of is that Penny has a key to the bar on her keychain, I saw her open up shop one time.

That night I watch Penny come in. She sets her bag down on the bar. She takes off her coat, I hear a little jingle when slides it off. Then she goes and hangs it up on the coat tree thing by the door."

"That was my chance. I took it."

"You took what."

"I took the key, went out for a smoke and got it copied at a chop shop down by the water. They work all night. Slipped back into the bar and dropped her keys in her pocket. Nobody noticed a thing."

"When did you steal the money?"

"That Friday night. It snowed, must have been a foot on the ground by the time the bar closed. Footprints everywhere people out to smoke and back in. Carlos closed up around three. I went back at four. There wasn't a soul on the street. It was perfect."

"What happened?"

"Bookie Sam leans on Carlos. No break in, no tampering. Looks bad for Carlos. There was this Vice cop named Cinco, on the bookie's payroll. Mostly to keep the police out of his hair, but Cinco did some muscle work too."

He hands the picture back to me, face down. He points to the handwriting. "Carlos wrote that. I guess he thought it was all taken care of that way. He should have run."

Madder's stories are as patterned as myths. I know what's coming. "Who killed him?"

"Cinco, probably. I know the murder cops eased up. I heard Cinco told them to keep out of his ongoing investigations. He was supposed to be breaking the dealers, but they were in his pocket too."

"But me, what I'm worried about is Penny. I'm afraid she saw me in her pockets, that she might put it all together. I know Cinco's been leaning on her a little to see if she knows where the money was. I mean, there's the message: don't fuck with the bookie's money. But the money isn't nothing, either."

"What happened to the money?"

"I gave Bonner enough to dig himself out. He left town a while, came back and said he'd hit it big at blackjack out west. Paid his debt. Year later I used mine to buy a building from Bonner's army buddy."

"Why'd you do it?"

"The money? I had to."

"Why?"

"He was married to my kid sister."

"And you got away with it."

"Seems that way."

"What happened with Penny. Why'd you stop worrying about her?"

"I took care of it."

"Did you pay her off?"

"No."

He's been grave since he started talking about Bonner but now his eyes narrow as the corner of his smile rises. "I wasn't going to give that bitch my money. I took her on a walk she didn't come back from."

I'm shaking my head, my hands are quivering. If I believe him now, I'm sitting two feet away from a man who killed someone, and there's nothing to say I might not die here. Now I know why the chills came down the back of my neck. And still, I can't stop.

"Which ones are the lies," I ask.

But he's done with me, leaving me as unsatisfied as all the men he owes and all the women he ran out on. He stands up and I flinch. "You got what you came for yet?"

I look at the door.

"That's right honey, you get on out of here and start minding your business."

Absurdly, I'm grasping for some gesture of closure, a handshake, I stand paralyzed.

His face goes cruel, "Get the fuck out," he snarls.

He slams the door behind me as I step across the threshold, I can feel the displaced air. I race outside and sprint around the corner. The daylight is dazzling. I hadn't realized how dark it was in there. There's a little alley. I take a few steps away from the sidewalk and retch into the alley's gutter.

When the dizziness fades, I wipe the sourness from the corner of my mouth and I walk up the street, faster now, but not fast enough to stand out from the sidling locals. I don't know what to believe, I'm in a madman's world, everything is true at once.

I find the fire inspector's number in my phone, the one who moved south. "I'm a reporter," I remind him. "We spoke last month."

"Okay, sure. What now."

"Who was the perp that you couldn't prosecute?"

"Are you kidding?"

"Maybe I can make it come out right now. It's part of a bigger story," I lie.

"Sweetheart, it was a dirty cop. You're getting nowhere with that."

"Just a name."

"No way," he says, and hangs up.

A dirty cop. Cinco. My head is light with Madder's lies and I feel sorrow welling up in my gut. The story is over, and it has no resolution, and I am left with only my losses again. I have to sit down. There's a church on the corner. I go in and slide into one of the back pews, slack against the praying wood. I hold my face in my hands and feel the tears running between my fingers. People come to cry in churches, repentance, guilt, sorrow. This is what they're here for. I hear a few old women coming and going, I hear their steps and their low whispers. They give me a wide berth. When the tears stop, I find the bathroom and splash water on my face. I put on sunglasses to hide my swollen eyes and walk back outside. I go down into the subway. I'm going home.

I sleep. I dream of teenagers looming in the distance, coming closer, closing in on me. I wake just as they descend upon me, birds of prey. It feels all too real, not a dream but a curse. I don't want to be alone. I call Jimmy, but the phone just rings into the night.

When I go out in the morning, the block is deserted, maybe it's too early, or too cold. Winter is clearing the streets. The corner boys have taken their business underground, their lookouts are gone from the bodega steps. The few people I see walk with their head down against the winds that rush at them, or the winds that are rumored to come. The streets hold no warmth. I get on the subway to go to Natalie's. Even here, the life is drained out of the riders. They burrow into their coats and scarves. They are insulated from each other as well as the cold. Nobody casts a searching glance. Nobody exchanges a nod.

Standing outside Natalie's building, I start to imagine telling her the story. I harbored a secret, even as I demanded her help. I've betrayed her, and there is Jimmy too in the weight of my guilt. I've violated them both. I turn around and go home.

The day should be warming but it doesn't. The air is bitter and dry. Back on the block, there's a man crouched down by the church parking lot, where a tribe of cats holds sway, either stalking the open ground, or perched like sentinels near the gate. The man is heavily bundled against the cold, but there's something off about him, a raggedness. He is unkempt in a way that suggests hard times. He has been still, crouched for a long minute before he reaches his bare fingers under the bottom of the chain link fence. He waits. The cats approach, and seeing he has no food to offer, retreat. He waits. One of them rubs up against the fence and then passes by and licks the man's fingers, a throwaway gesture as the cat moves on to perch on an old tire. The man turns to me, he has known all along I was watching. "They make me happy," he says. "You know?"

At home I crawl back under the covers. Somewhere along the way I must have convinced myself as I convinced the others, that my brother lay at the end of the line. That I would find him saved. But now the search has ended, and I am left with the world. The pangs of withdrawal and the deeper thing that is no longer numbed. I recognize this feeling. It's what I ran away from a year ago. It's a broken heart.

FOLLOW ME DOWN

12.

NOW, THE CITY that has been my solace turns against me. I close the doors on the world and take refuge in the night, in dreams.

My lover calls, and though for the first time I crave his embrace, I let it ring. Natalie calls, and I let it ring, and finally I cannot stand my own refusals anymore. I drag the suitcase out from under my bed. I fold my clothes into it. I am doing what I am good at, that's what I tell myself. I sit one last time in the warmth of the sunny kitchen and stare out the back window, past the roof of the chop shop, past the windowless factory and its decaying wooden water tower. A train slips across the elevated tracks a mile away.

At the subway steps, there's a familiar fat man calling out for change. He puts down his begging cup and helps me carry the suitcase down. I give him a twenty. He looks at it and shrugs. "You're not coming back, are you," he says.

I ride under the river and drag the suitcase up the steps. No one helps me now. Halfway down the side street, I sit on a stranger's stoop to rest. The city is just waking up, people are cradling cups of coffee, walking dogs. Two young men stroll toward me. They're in dirty jeans, plain thick hoodies, they have the chalky hands of laborers. But everything about them is elegant, they're speaking another language, maybe it's Greek, I'm not sure. Their faces are framed by loose dark curls. Each man leans back into his gait, every step as languid and sensual as the long vowels that trail off at the ends of their sentences. I let them pass by and then I walk behind them for a long time, listening to their lullaby voices, understanding nothing.

When I arrive at the train station, I put headphones on and turn the volume up as loud as I can bear. I ride the long escalator down, and wait at the edge of the crowd. Most of them are standing still, looking at their phones. A few are talking over the general din of the massive space, I see their mouths moving but the music in my ears blots out their words. If I looked up, I'd see the big board with its plastic numbers clicking to show the trains and their departing gates. But I don't. I watch the crowd, and suddenly it swarms over toward one of the doorways. I follow them down another long escalator, deep underground to where the train waits. I find a seat and close my eyes. It will be a long time before I open them again, not until the train has cleared the city. I don't have a ticket but that's all right. I don't want to know where it's going.

FOLLOW ME DOWN

Acknowledgments

I consider it my great good luck to be part of Red Lemonade, and I thank Richard Nash for his brilliance, his energy, and his judicious red pen. Thanks also to my agent Sally Wofford-Girand for her shepherding, and to Ian Crowther for the wonderful cover.

For longstanding encouragement, close readings, and generative conversations, I'm grateful to Jodi Baker, Carlos Blackburn, Rachel Devlin, Neil Freeman, Fred Scharmen, Kevin Slavin, Jonathan Taylor, Genya Turovsky, and my mother, Meryl Stark. Benjamin Kilgust, Sherri Wasserman, and Ritchie Williams also chimed in on an early draft of this book.

I started writing about this city and these streets on my blog, Municipal Archive. My readers have given me the gift of their enthusiasm and comments, for which I owe them immeasurable thanks.

There is an entry under every letter of the alphabet in the encyclopedia of my gratitude to Bre Pettis. He sparks and shelters me, he has my heart.

Kio Stark lives in Brooklyn, NY. *Follow Me Down* is her first novel.